SPECTRAL VISIONS: GRIM FAIRY TALES

EDITED BY
COLIN YOUNGER

WITH

A FOREWORD
BY
IAIN ROWAN

Dedicated to Steve Watts

Many thanks to 'Steve the Reiver' for helping us make our Spectral Visions into realities.
We the Visionaries salute you!

Spectral Visions Press
spectralvisionspress@sunderland.ac.uk

Spectral Visions
spectralvisions@sunderland.ac.uk

ACKNOWLEDGEMENTS

The Editor would like to thank the contributors to this volume both for the excellence of their contributions and for the patience they have displayed while this book has come to fruition. Special thanks to the student employees of Spectral Visions Press and in particular Stephanie Gallon and Jamie Spears for their copy editing skills and their tireless dedication to the project. Also thanks are due to Sam Morrell and Katie Watson for their extreme drive, willingness and ability to motivate others. With thanks to the editing team: Jen Bell, Sarah Butler, Emily Crosby, Shannon Crozier, Jane Currie, Chelsea Dalby, Sophie Delacoe, Connor Lancaster, Lauren O'Dell, Vasilki Mallikourti and Gabrielle Swales under the leadership of Nicola Rooks and Jenah Colledge; the proof-reading team: Sacha Margetson, Emma Richardson and Danielle Shaw led by Kate Edmonds and Michelle McCabe and the typesetting team: Emily Bird, Daniel Farrell and Pauline Messer led by Jennie Watson. Our final and extreme thanks go to David Newton for media and book cover design, Katie Loyd for her exquisitely, wicked illustrations, Iain Rowan for the fairy-tale forward and Steve Watts for his unerring support.

Figure 1 Lady Bird

CONTENTS

List of Illustrations	viii
Foreword – Iain Rowan	ix

Traditional

The Story of Iron Henry – John Strachan	2
The Tale of the Black Knight & the White Princess – Mike Adamson	3
Midnight – Ashleigh Hallimond	11
The Princess and the Pea – Charlotte Haley	16
The Witch of Hardknot Pass – Jade Diamond	20
Reverie – Joseph Brash	24

Northern Nightmares

Once upon a Tyne – Colin Younger	29
Dragon – Michelle McCabe	32

Not so Snow White

Choke – Sophie Raine	39
An Overturned Tale – Emily Bird	46

On Giants and Trolls

The Huldrefolk – Alison Younger	51
From the Sky – Glen Supple	62
Jack the Giant Butcher – Gary McKay	69

Tales from the Hood

A Family Dinner – Janet Cooper	76
Red Riding Blood	80
Sweet Red – Jennie Watson	84
Wolfbann – Stephanie Gallon	90

Supernatural

The Tree – James Christian Strachan	93
Hannah Smith – Mulier Maris	98
The Ghost Who Died – Alex Milne	99
Love and Death – Emma Collingwood	105
The Baroness and the Servant Girl – E.L Little-Gainford	109
The Glass Coffin – Daniel Farrell	115

The Elfin-song – Joshua Wray	119
Cast Down Your Eyes – Jamie Spears	126
beauty, lies, sleeping – Bill Hughes	128
The Natural Order of Things – Barry Hall	131
Fear Little Piggy – Laura Kremmel	133
Evil-Alice – Jenah Colledge	138
Ruins – Andrea Bowd	140
Notes on Contributors	142

LIST OF ILLUSTRATIONS

Figure 1 Lady Bird	v
Figure 2 Radgie	x
Figure 3 Iron Henry	1
Figure 4 Demon Pea	15
Figure 5 Vicious Vegetable	19
Figure 6 Spectral Visions	23
Figure 7 Hangin' Around	27
Figure 8 Roarie battles the RedCaps	28
Figure 9 Gadgie	30
Figure 10 Radgie Revisited	29
Figure 11 Lambton Worm	37
Figure 12 Five Dwarves	38
Figure 13 … The Other Two	45
Figure 14 Necronomicon	49
Figure 15 The Huldrefolk	50
Figure 16 Huldrekarl	61
Figure 17 Evil Beanstalk	68
Figure 18 Wolf in Red's Clothing	75
Figure 19 Red's Ahead	83
Figure 20 Spanner in the Works	89
Figure 21 Evil Tree	91
Figure 22 Doppleganger Fairy	92
Figure 23 Tooth Demon	97
Figure 24 The Sorcerer	125
Figure 25 Carnivorous Porkers	132
Figure 26 Extreme Piggy Close-up	137
Figure 27 Evil Alice	139
Figure 28 Memento Mori	141
Figure 29 Madness	142

FOREWORD

IAIN ROWAN

We are the stories that we tell ourselves. We are the stories that other people tell about us (or that we *believe* that they tell about us, which is a different thing altogether). Our society is shaped by the stories and narratives that are told about it.

Sometimes those stories are fairy tales.

Grim(m), cautionary tales that tell us to watch our steps and follow the rules or something will come for us and we won't like it. Stories that tell us not to walk through the woods, at least not on this night, and under that moon. Fairy tales teach us that sometimes you follow all the rules, you stick to the path, you don't stray into the forest or sleep on that particular grassy hill, you do what mother and father tell you, and you don't speak to strangers…but one day on a lonely path there they are anyway, waiting for you. Fairy tales remind us that life itself is arbitrary and capricious and appeasing it, for a while, is the best that we can do. The fairy stories that we tell ourselves are full of wonder but also full of dread, and some of the puckish folk that populate them are all spite and scheming, Lilith's children who know their place: above us.

Neil Gaiman wrote (paraphrasing GK Chesterton) that *'fairy tales are more than true: not because they tell us that dragons exist, but because they tell us that dragons can be beaten.'* He's right, and that's a good thing to know. You *can* tweak the dragon's tail and run away to live happily ever after. But on the other hand, sometimes they eat you.

For writers, there are other kinds of stories that we tell ourselves. Writing is something that someone else can do, not me. There are no new stories left to write, everything has been said. I'll never be a writer. Rejection means give up. I am no good at this. Other people are better. No one will want to read this. I should give up.

The authors whose work you will read here come from across the UK and indeed, across the world. Many of them are students of creative writing, at the University of Sunderland (home of Spectral Visions) or elsewhere, and one of the most valuable things such programmes can do is to support students in telling themselves a *different* set of stories. I can write, and I will write. I have stories to tell. I can improve. I will persist. I will develop and grow. I will keep writing and I will get rejected and I will go back and write more. I have stories to tell, and I can tell them.

You see the results here: vivid re-imaginings of the traditional fairy tale from cultures familiar and unfamiliar, explorations of new and exciting approaches to the form, poetry and prose and illustration. The stories in this collection explore the many echoes between the traditional fairy tale and the gothic: the uncanny, the grotesque and the fear of darkness, death and worlds unknown seeping through it all like rot through damp timber.

Welcome to *Spectral Visions: Grim Fairy Tales*. You may think that you have spent just minutes reading this collection, only to put it down and discover that a whole day has passed. That's fairyland for you.

Figure 2 Radgie

Traditional

Figure 3 Iron Henry

The Story of Iron Henry

John Strachan

Iron Henry's on the floor
His little eyes a-staring.
They never seem to close at all,
Angry, fierce, and glaring.

He never asked to be like this,
For once he used to be a prince,
But he refused a witch's kiss,
So he's been yellow ever since.

He never asked to be so small
His heart so full of venom.
To look so gross to one and all,
And especially to women.

Trapped inside a yellow skin,
Iron Henry, look at him.
No lover, friend, or family kin
If someone only could save him.

He sits close by a deep dark pond
In a walléd garden lonely.
He thinks of all that once was fond,
If only, if only, if only.

But then he sees her walking by,
A vision of fair beauty.
Tall and blonde, she seems so high,
Though also rather snooty.

A golden ball lies in her hand
In it she'll see her husband,
But then jumps up the froggy fond,
And she drops it in the pond.

He looks into the princess's eyes,
And his eyes they plead and call,
But she takes him in her dainty hand,
And throws him at the wall.

His brains they're now all dashéd out,
And his blood it flows right down.
The Princess gives a happy pout
And readjusts her crown.

His blood slips into the magic pond,
And he's suddenly re-formed.
And the princess haughty, tall and blond,
Sees a handsome prince transformed.

'Now, this is better than a frog!'
Thinks the princess all agog,
'How glad I am I did not miss!'
And she gives him love's true kiss.

The Tale of the Black Knight and the White Princess

Mike Adamson

Once upon a time …

In the land of Galeotheria, there lived a Black Knight. A great warrior in black armour, with black shield and pennants, who was known throughout the land as invincible, the very hand of fate, for when he rode forth from his black castle he brought in his train all human suffering. Pillage and war were but the outward manifestation of fear, famine and disease, and the people whispered of him in the dead of night when long years had gone by, saying, 'soon the Black Knight shall ride once more, and the gods have mercy upon us when he does.'

Mercy indeed, for who can stay the hand of destiny? But hope burns eternal in the human heart, if oft tainted with greed, vanity and ego, and when the hand of terror came amongst the people always there would be those who would challenge him. The strongest knights, the mightiest egos, each would claim the right of saving Galeotheria from the tyranny of his rampage, and covering themselves in glory thereby.

But the Black Knight was undefeated. One by each, the kingdom's strongest hands fell to his overwhelming charge, to his mindless rampage, and the vitality of the land was sapped away, life by life and hope by hope, until all that remained was the stoicism to endure the inevitability of his return.

The King of Galeotheria was an old man. Old, and saddened by his inability to change this destiny, and his health was fading with his days. His house was faltering, and the ancient line of his ancestors was nearing its end. Soon there would be struggle for the throne, and he could but smile for the responsibility of ruling this land in such an age was a burden coveted only by fools.

Fools the world had aplenty; and the great wheel of history would turn as surely as day followed night.

The king was without a son, but to him had come a fine daughter, the fair Princess Myrjana. Many would court her, and the sons of noble houses saw their fortunes in wedding their blood to the ancient and still-respected line of kings. But while Myrjana had cultivated the virtues of a princess, she had also honoured her father's silent wish, that he had had a son, by training with the finest instructors of the army in the arts of horsemanship and combat. She was known to be a match for most any in the saddle, with the bow, the sword and even the lance, and those close to her sensed her frustration as her father's days grew as short as the coming of the Black Knight. These tragedies would surely strike together, and as the days of autumn turned to winter and the trees became as skeletons to the harsh north wind, Myrjana spent her days introverted, brooding on cruel fates she could not avert.

She would stand swathed in furs on the high walls of the castle, staring off into the eye of the wind, as if seeking the enemy beyond the vales of her people, knowing if any were to resist his coming, it must be soon. She had heard the bragging in the halls, but knew in her heart that this time none would go forth. There seemed no point, and as days grew harsh simple preservation loomed large in the hearts of those to whom such task would fall.

But as the days shortened and the sun was seen less frequently, and the people settled to endure life's lowest ebb, word reached the castle of a stranger, a wandering wise man who had journeyed from the grey north with words of comfort to the ordinary people.

He spoke of the coming winter and of its personification, the dark shadow that waited at the back of every mind, and he told them to fear not.

Myrjana was fascinated to hear this man speak, but while she could have ordered him brought to the royal hall, she knew such a command may colour his words. So she dressed in the robes of a commoner and with but two similarly-disguised guards went forth into the town one cold and windy evening.

He was found in a tavern by the river, nursing ale as the fires fought the chill, and many had gathered to hear him. He seemed in no way special, a man of middle age wrapped in simple grey robes, but when he spoke it was with a forthrightness that encouraged belief. 'Let the good and the bad alike come to thee,' he said, 'and weigh each, for each has a value. The good we may easily understand, but the bad we may profit from if we are but wise enough to see the lessons it brings.'

'How do we learn from murder and destruction?' a man asked, his hands upraised. 'What lesson does sorrow bring we could not learn some other way?'

'Only in extremis does the human soul burn brightest,' the prophet said gently. 'In such times do we see valour, both of the sword and of the humblest heart. And for all its might, evil cannot taint these things, though it should triumph, and so, by this truth, does it fail.'

Some would have dismissed him as a peddler of platitudes, but in the warm, smoky shadows, where Myrjana sat cradling ale, a voice spoke, strong and plain. 'When the darkness rides forth, what should we do? Is it best to defy the gale, foreknowing defeat, or to cringe at the blow, knowing just as surely it shall come?'

The prophet smiled softly at this and thought a moment. 'Honour and nobility are things of human making. They govern our behaviour, and they place value on how we go to our fate. If it salves the heart to die fighting, then die fighting. If it fouls the soul to stand silent amongst one's fellows, praying only that another shall step forth, then reject this. But at all costs, remember: the darkness and the light are in flux, and as day follows night evil shall no more triumph in eternity than good shall be free of its shadow.' He hunched forward in the firelight, the flames playing leaping glimmers across his weather-beaten face. 'We await the One who shall deny the darkness, the one who shall understand what this foe is, does and needs to be, and send it back to the anonymity of simple balance.' He shrugged, looked around the room, and raised his tankard. 'It may be you, traveller. Or you.' His gaze moved on, and lingered upon Myrjana, where her features were obscured in shadow. 'Or you.'

Difficult thoughts swirled in her mind that night, and in the days that followed, and she warred with his words. Fear was her companion, and the images he had drawn were a torment to a brave heart.

'Shall none defend my people?' Myrjana would whisper to herself, or fling in rhetorical tirade at others, as the smoky halls resounded to song and bluster, yet no warrior would declare his stand. 'This kingdom may as well climb into its grave, for if hope is lost, all is lost.'

'Noble words are easily spoken,' she heard muttered behind her back once, 'by one whom honour shall never call upon to make good.'

Perhaps it was this dismissal that made the fire blossom within her, or her father slipping into insensibility that same night, but when the first rumours reached the castle of a dark terror in the north, it was Myrjana who made declaration that the realm would be defended.

Knights and warriors were scornful, or shamed by their own inaction, but remained affixed to their drinking halls by the spectre of certain defeat, and it was with her own scorn that the princess called for her horse and armour.

The aged Queen begged for her to reconsider, and wept for the fall of her house and line in this folly, but Myrjana's path was foretold and she was resolute.

In grey dawn she was dressed in the finest armour the craftsmen of Galeotheria could build, and her warhorse saddled in the trappings of the royal house. Her lance streamed the banner of the king and the pennants of her helm were the colours of her line since ages past. Without fanfare did she ride out, into stormy skies over the fells and moors, as if going forth into the cold grave of history while breath remained, for none she left behind ever thought to see her living again.

The Black Knight was abroad in the world, and Galeotheria tensed before the blow of his brutal mace. As the first snow touched the earth Myrjana passed those on the road who spoke of terror in the night, and she spurred on into the teeth of winter.

Three days journey brought her to the first sign of his hand, and she reined in amongst tumbled dwellings and burning thatch where a hamlet had stood, forlorn in a wooded vale. Blood in the snow mingled with the prints of great hooves, and she knew she had found him.

She eased her cloak, drew on her helmet and put her head back to cry with all her might into the lowering overcast, 'I call you out, messenger of darkness! You come against my land, but you shall not go unopposed! Come forth and face justice!'

The angry sky mocked her words, racing clouds seemed to whisper of the helplessness of mortal flesh, and for terrible moments she felt the Black Knight would not deign even to recognise her challenge. But of such is human doubt made, and this foe had more substance. She felt it first as a tremble in the earth, her fair pony shying as he sensed something evil. His ears lay back and he scented the wind, his heart pounding as he knew battle beckoned.

From out the grey haze of the softly fluttering snow came a shadow. Something huge moved in the gloom, and resolved slowly to the shape of a mounted warrior... A black warrior on a black steed, black pennants streaming from his helm, and a black lance carried in a mailed fist. The thud of hooves came like drumbeats through the ground, and Myrjana's heart rose into her mouth as she beheld this terrible spectacle.

Its voice was like the rumble of thunder amongst the high slopes. 'Who calls upon the Dark? Who dares challenge?'

Summoning her courage, Myrjana raised her own lance so the banner of the king was tugged in the wind. 'I, Myrjana, Princess of Galeotheria, do call out the scourge and challenge you to battle.' Her voice seemed thin and flat in the biting air, she admitted to herself her words sounded pitiful, and she was not surprised to hear laughter like a distant rockslide.

'Return to your halls, warm your hands. I have not come for you.'

'But it is through me that you shall pillage!' she returned with venom. 'I stand Protector of my people, and with my dying breath shall I do so!'

The monstrous figure sat immobile for a long moment. 'You shall,' was the grunted reply, before great spurs struck home and the warhorse pranced.

Myrjana was struck speechless as the Black Knight exploded into a charge like thunder, and she saw his monstrous shape coming down upon her. With a dry mouth she brought her lance down into the nook of her shield and spurred her mount. *This is impossible*, she thought. *The knights were right to decline the bait of honour...* But as she drove at the oncoming monster she remembered the prophet, and saw for just an instant her own light in stark relief against the enemy's darkness, and a strange peace flooded through her. *What comes shall be endured; what we may change, we shall.*

The Black Knight was undefeated in all the long years of his reign of terror, and Myrjana almost felt his palpable amazement as she went under the thrust of his lance, the point skating off the upper edge of her shield, and her own weapon shattered against his breastplate. They whipped by each other as she cast away the haft and snatched up her second from the loops by her right stirrup, and glanced back. She had not unseated the enemy, but she had shaken him, and that was more encouraging than all the words she had ever heard.

The Black Knight paused and shook his head slowly, calling across twenty yards. 'You do not imagine you can possibly defeat me?'

'I am not here to commit suicide,' she taunted, almost breathless with the surge of her own courage.

'But you are,' was the grunted dismissal, before he crashed into the charge again.

Myrjana rose to the fight, came at him with all her strength and ability, but she knew she had had all the luck there would be. He had seen her advantage in smaller stature and would compensate. This time his lance took her in the shoulder, a vast impact that tore away the outer protective shell and twisted her savagely, almost punching her from her horse's back. But her second lance splintered home squarely in the giant's middle and his bellow of pain and rage assaulted her ears. As they went by she saw the shocking gleam of redness where her lance had parted the plates of his armour and torn through mail and jerkin to the flesh beneath.

So you can be hurt! she thought savagely, her exultation clouding the wave of pain from her shoulder. Her shield was suddenly almost too heavy to hold as her arm spasmed and became numb, and she propped it against her thigh as she tore free her sword and wheeled it over her head. 'Come! Come to your death, accursed giant!'

The Black Knight came on again as if the wound meant nothing, bellowing like a wild beast, and his lance came for her heart as the pigeon finds home. She twisted at the last moment, her pony shied from the bigger horse, and the lance skated across her shield. In the same moment she wheeled the long sword and took the pennants from his helmet, her laughter a sneer at him. He roared his fury, cast away his lance and drew a broadsword as long as she stood tall.

They turned short, wheeled and she avoided the crashing stroke that would have broken her shield arm, to feint high, teasing his shield up … then struck low, under the arc of black, probing for the red mess at his side. Her blade hacked home, exploited the damage and found flesh once more, but that was all skill and strength could manage. His back-stroke jarred her shield, crushed her arm back against her body and half lifted her from her horse. It was all she could do to not drop her sword, and she knew when flight was in order.

Gasping for breath in the icy air, she gave her pony his head to gallop in the wooded valley, and heard the thunder of mighty hooves behind her. But what small size lacked in strength, great size lacked in speed, and she stayed ahead of him, weaving through the trees, cutting back and forth as fir branches whipped at her faceplate and flayed at the trappings that fluttered over her plate armour.

Yet that monstrous shadow, the night to her day, was without fatigue, and wounds seemed to slow him none, while her pony was tiring and she knew her own strengths were almost expended. *Use what you have, use what your enemy does not have,* she thought, remembering the words of her instructors long ago.

Day follows night. The words of the prophet were with her in that moment as she saw the blackness behind her, and she knew that in this instant, night followed day. And all became clear in that split second.

She wheeled for the lower slope of the valley and her pony made ground downhill as the heavy horse lunged to follow, and she made the mouth of a small gully she knew with a few lengths to spare. As she plunged into it she heard the giant laugh as he assumed she had sealed her fate, and he reined back to merely follow her... to the blank end of the gully, where a stream was already freezing to a cascade of icicles.

She reined back and unhooked her feet from the stirrups, to drop to the ground and slap her pony, sending him on through an overhang of rock below the frozen stream, and with the drumming hoof-beats in her ears she turned at last.

The Black Knight seemed to fill the gully, rising impossibly huge. His mount reared, lofting his helm twelve feet high like the upraised fist of doom, and when the great hooves came down the ground shook. He sat tall for a long moment as she merely stood, waiting, then he kicked out of his stirrups and slid down to step through the fresh whiteness, one stride after another until he towered over her, over seven feet tall.

She glared up at the vision slit, seeking his eyes, but there were none to find, and she wondered if there was anything living within that terrible shell... But blood was blood and she knew what she must do. She let her shield go, fall to the icy ground at her side, and she held her arm close as if injured. The giant breathed, she saw vapour around his faceshield, and knew he was merely waiting.

Her sword slipped from her fingers, falling into the dirt and fresh snow by her feet, and she forced up her face guard so her breath plumed in the cold.

'Why?' the giant asked, a deep rumble.

'Why do any stand up for all they hold dear?' she returned, her voice trembling. 'This time the crop of valiants was found wanting, and it fell to me.'

'Courage is noble,' the giant breathed. 'The death-struggle of any being is often its finest hour, but the end ... is the end.'

She sneered at him, trembling with fatigue and cold. 'Finish it. Let it be over.'

The Black Knight dropped his shield to the snow and shrugged faintly. 'As you wish,' he grunted, and hefted his sword two-handed, to wheel it high for the death-blow.

Myrjana flinched low and the mighty stroke found the frozen overhang of the stream, bit the ice deep and lodged fast. Hooking a toe under her blade, Myrjana flicked it up into her hands and stepped forward with a cry of strength, to drive it with every ounce of her venom for the ragged wound at his side.

His bellow was enough to wake the dead as the blade drove home, and he toppled backward like a falling tree. His great horse skittered away from him, snorting and distressed, and Myrjana stood panting as she saw the mailed hands take the blade in a tenacious grip. 'You cannot win,' was the grunted defiance, and the blade began to ease from the wound. But she put her metal-shod foot to the hilt and drove the point clean through to the metal beyond, and at last the giant's hands fell away as his body moved convulsively to his breathing.

'You cannot win,' he repeated. 'Though you take my life, the wheel turns.'

'And the time has come for it to turn away from all you represent,' she said softly as she crouched by him.

'You are dying, strange man. Why do you plague my kingdom?'

'As well ask the sun why it rises. I am part of you.'

'Never!' But as she spoke, Myrjana realised he was right. That was the prophet's meaning.

'Yes,' the giant whispered now. 'You understand at last. To defeat all you hate you must become that very thing. You realise now that there is a tiny spark of me in you.'

'As there is... Must be... Of me in your foul heart,' Myrjana whispered. She reached trembling hands to unlatch his visor and raise it, fearing all she might look upon, but was faintly disappointed. He was but a man, of broad, powerful features, clean-shaven, not unhandsome, and his pale blue eyes were glazing now as the wound did its work. The redness at his side had spilled upon the fresh white, and his lips were showing blue.

'What can you tell me from this threshold at which you stand?' Myrjana asked.

'Nothing,' he replied, strangely calm. 'That is not my role.' He closed his eyes. 'What shall you be without me?'

'Free,' she breathed as she rose to look down on him.

The Black Knight passed into history in that gully, and Myrjana took his helmet back with her as token of her victory. His body was found by scouts, and burned in the town square below the castle walls, as the people cheered with one voice. The pretenders stepped back, as Myrjana was crowned Queen of Galeotheria, Lady Protector of the Realm, and the line of kings was remade.

The prophet's words had come true, for day had followed night, and the light had restored balance to darkness out of control. The sunrise had come for a new age, and the kingdom rejoiced.

But in all the years of her reign, Myrjana perhaps alone understood truly the consequences of her actions, for each blessing she brought upon her people, each prosperity they enjoyed, had its price, and a day would come when payment was due.

Twenty years of peace and justice succeeded the horrors of the dark time, until the Black Knight was but a memory, and Queen Myrjana passed into the lore of the land as the Grand Monarch. And she alone was unsurprised when rumours grew of something in the cold north, something sinister that stirred with a malice half-forgotten, and looked with malevolent eyes upon Galeotheria. But she did not fear it, for it was an old, old friend.

The twilight had come at last.

MIDNIGHT

ASHLEIGH HALLIMOND

I never could have imagined I would attend a ball as grand as this. Girls like me didn't get to go to places like this. We didn't get the beautiful dresses, or the frivolous glass shoes that looked fabulous but weren't particularly practical in any sense or form. Still, walking in those shoes down the black onyx stairs into the ball felt like a dream.

A man, wearing a crisp midnight blue suit, waited for me at the bottom. The festivities had already begun, but I was not bothered by that fact. The other guests waltzed between each other beautifully, their clothes twinkling under the soft glowing candlelight. A man waited at the bottom in a crisp midnight blue suit.

He bowed his head and smiled. 'You must be the girl my footman spoke of. You look beautiful.' He took my hand and kissed it gently.

I blushed. 'Your friend was very kind to invite me here.'

'I'm glad that you appreciate it, though I must admit I am rather thankful myself. Would you care to dance?'

'I must thank you; the dress and the shoes are beautiful. It was very kind of you to give them to me.'

'Our friend said that you needed help to get out of the life you were in. I felt obliged to assist.' He leaned in to murmur in my ear. 'And you look truly beautiful in that dress.'

'I still can't believe I'm here. It's like a dream. I never thought I'd be able to get out of that place.'

'You weren't happy with your family?'

I huffed out a laugh and looked away. 'I don't think you can call them a family. My father died and I was left with his wife. She wasn't particularly fond of me. I cooked and cleaned, and lived on the floor.'

'That must have been difficult.'

'It was. That is why I'm so thankful for this opportunity. Even a moment of freedom is better in a lifetime of slavery.'

'Well, I am glad that my ball could help you with it.'

We spun, his arm locked around my waist in such a grip that I thought I might bruise where he held me. We barely spoke, letting the minutes fade around us.

His grin stayed in place as we continued around the room. 'I hope you realise this is all your doing.' He whispered, pulling me closer to him. Our chests were touching now, his face so close to mine I could feel every exhaled breath, like a feather gliding across my skin. Something felt different in that moment, how he spoke, how he looked. Something had changed.

'Everyone is here for you,' he moved, pushing me to arm's length, before spinning me back in so that he held me from behind.

We looked out onto the other guests, people I'd never met, people who'd never have glanced my way before. They wore beautiful gowns of silk and satin; bold, bright dresses of luscious reds in so many shades that when they twirl in amongst one another the colours appeared to be the only things that mattered. I couldn't stop looking at those spinning colours.

'Take a look for yourself,' he breathed in my ear. 'Really look, what do you see?'

I looked. All of the spinning and twirling was just what we'd been doing. It was a ball, and these people were dancing; what more could it be? 'I see couples, just like us.'

He tightened his hands around my waist, and rested his chin on my shoulder. I'd never been as close to someone before, and it felt strange, yet oddly comforting. 'You're looking, but you're not truly seeing,' he whispered. 'Look again.'

Hands. There was something wrong with their hands. I watched them carefully. Their fingers tangled. No. Not tangled. Their fingers were sewn together. The man couldn't help but clasp his hand around her waist, the same way the woman couldn't help but hold his shoulder. Someone had sewn the partners together to make them in a perfect hold position.

'I couldn't host a ball without any guests now could I? They're all here for you. This was your wish.'

'This isn't what I wanted,' I made an attempt to pull away from him, but his hands held me in place.

'Oh, but it is.' He spun me back so I face him once more. His eyes burned with delight. 'You wanted to run away, get away from those you believed to have forced you into a life of solitude and slavery. You were ungrateful, taking their house and their hearth, but never thankful for it.'

We started spinning gracefully in and amongst the sewn together people. 'The dead dance for you and you alone, my dear. We can waltz to your heart's content, and they will follow us. They are mine to command, but here for your pleasure.' His fingers stroked my cheek with a delicate touch. 'Don't you see what I'm giving you?'

I pulled away from him, but he held tight to my waist. This man had seemed like answer to my prayers; but now he had the devil in his eyes. I looked around once more, taking in the sewn-together monstrosities. At first I'd only noticed their hands, but there was more to it than that. Their eyes were hollowed out; just these sockets of emptiness. Even their skin didn't look right now that I took full notice of it. It looked yellowed and weathered, like old parchment left in the sun.

'It's interesting what you see when you really look, isn't it?' he said menacingly.

'Why have you done this? I didn't ask for *this*. I only wanted to leave that place.'

Our hands dropped as I took a few steps away from him, and the room was consumed with a sudden stillness as the music stopped. I glanced around and everyone turned in our direction; their empty gazes filled me with dread.

'My dear, you could have left long before our friend gave you the opportunity to do so; you chose to put your trust in someone you'd just met. You foolishly believed that *I* would make all your little dreams come true?' He chuckled, his eyes watching me with a wicked and dark intent.

'I didn't know.'

'You didn't *ask*.'

'I didn't expect you to control things like this.'

He strode toward me, grabbing my hips and pulling me in. The mask of charm and perfection he wore was starting to crack, revealing a picture of cruelty. His left hand grabbed at my hair. I flinched.

'You truly thought that a ball would change your life?' he sneered. 'You are desperate to be given things you do not deserve.'

'I want to go home now.'

A change coursed through the air, and the floor moved. I screamed in pain as the glass shoes shrank and squeezed my feet.

I tried to pull away, but he held me sure and close. I could feel the glass moving, melting and bubbling against my now blistered feet. 'Let me go. Please.'

'You think you have a choice now? You said that you'd give anything to leave that place; by accepting my servant's help, you parted with your soul. It's mine, my dear, mine to have and mine to do with as I please.'

The melting glass of my shoes cooled instantly, trapping my feet in prisons of glass. 'So I'm here for the rest of my life?'

'That all depends on you. Though you may still be a pathetic creature…your desire for greatness, is something I would like to see by my side.'

'I have no desire to be great. Why can't you see that my only desire was to get out from that awful place?'

He snorted, derisively. He let go of one of my hands and dusted something off his sleeve. 'You no longer wanted to be a servant to the family who kept you out of the cold. You thought you deserved better.'

'That doesn't mean that I wished for greatness.'

'You believed that you could convince me to rescue you from that life you hated so much. To make someone save you, you must believe you deserve to be saved. You must believe in your own greatness; you must believe that you can in fact make me want you.'

'Your friend said you could help me out of my situation.'

'And I can. But this is about the darkness in your heart.'

'There is no darkness in my heart.'

'If that were true, my friend would not have invited you here. There is untapped darkness within you; I can sense it. If we just let it blossom…'

I shifted uncomfortably and looked down to the floor. 'What do you want from me?'

The music started up, and his hands found my waist once more. Earlier, the night seemed as though it would never end; now it felt like it would last forever. 'I need someone who'd be willing to help me, to stay by my side and rule and command the dead.'

'I don't want to rule the dead.'

'You have a choice to make. You can get all you desire and more; but you'll have to work beside me, knowing all the horrors which lurk in the dark. You'll be the woman of shadows that children fear, the woman of beauty and darkness.' He stroked back my hair, and caressed the nape of my neck.

'I don't want to be a thing of nightmares. I want to leave. I thought getting away from there was what I wanted, but if this is the cost, I don't want to pay it.'

'I'm giving you what you need; don't be rude. You might not have expected this as your way out, but you know in your heart it's better.'

'The evil you see inside me will not come out. I will not help you.'

Letting go of my neck, he took up my hand once more. 'Then we will dance together one last time my queen that is not to be.'

In a room filled with swaying bodies, it was strange to feel so at ease for these moments of silence while I danced with the devil, but it was comforting. The song came to an end and I felt a burning sensation in my hands. An attempt to pull away just made it hurt more. His hands held mine harder, hundreds of tiny pinpricks bit into my skin all at the same time. 'If you won't be by my side, you will remain here for all eternity, Ella.' He smiled sadly. 'I wish you would have considered my offer more carefully.'

Our hands were sewn together just as the other guests' hands were. 'If you force me to dance, you'll be forced to dance with me.'

He shrugged. 'Perhaps.'

The flesh on his face began to bubble and drip, slowly melting away from his skull. I screamed in horror as one of the corpse's faces took its place: the eyeless face with the decrepit, yellowed skin.

Somewhere in the distance, a clock struck midnight.

Figure 4 Demon Pea

THE PRINCESS AND THE PEA

CHARLOTTE HALEY

In a land where the clouds were often darkened with coming storms and the sunshine was scarce, there lived a King and a Queen, both ageing rapidly and anxious for the continuation of their line. Their only offspring was a son who, though handsome, had no special accomplishments to boast of, spending most of his time roaming the ample rooms of the castle as though he had dreamt of finding some great treasure therein, and, in waking daylight, was resolved to find it. Though his parents had encouraged him to venture out into the kingdom he would soon rule, the Prince was reluctant to lend his attention to the villages surrounding them.

'If he does not find a princess to marry soon, we shall not have grandchildren to carry forth our blood,' said the King to the Queen.

'We must find him a princess—but not just any princess,' said the Queen. 'She must be a true princess. Her blood must be blue as a brooklet's water, her bones the finest porcelain.'

The next day, the Queen sent a letter to each of the surrounding kingdoms, requiring that each monarch should send to her their most beautiful and talented daughter (or their only daughter, if they had but one). The message was well-received, for it seemed that the other kings and queens were equally eager to marry off their children. The Prince received one princess a night, taking tea in the parlour where they would discuss uninteresting topics and fripperies—often did he have more curiosity in the crumbs of their cakes than the vapid conversation offered by these 'princesses'. Still, the Queen persisted in her search.

When the Prince grew tired and slumped up to his bed, the princess for that night would be led to her own chamber, where she would find no less than twenty mattresses, piled precariously upon twenty feather beds.

'Oh! What a high bed!' She would invariably exclaim, before climbing to the top, bereft of the knowledge that the Queen had hidden an uncooked pea in the folds of the bedding. If she was to awake with fatigue in her limbs, an ache in her back and sleepless eyes, due to the discomfort that pea had caused, the Queen would know that she had found the princess most deserving of her son's favour. But, alas! None of the princesses who had entered the castle missed one wink of sleep while staying there. The Prince, scorning his mother's desperate attempt to find him a mate, went to the King.

'Father, won't you stop these agonising trials? I would rather live eternally and carry on your bloodline than marry one of these insipid trollops!' his petulant voice rang in the King's ears and he was soon asked to leave by the bottle of gin gripped in his father's claw.

When the last of the princesses had come and gone, without the slightest complaint of disturbed slumber, the Queen fell into a deep depression dreaming of the grandchildren she would never hold, who would never kiss her cheek. The King tried to comfort his wife with gifts and affection, yet nothing seemed to sate her starving misery. Mimicking her gloom was the weather, overcome with bouts of torrential rain and violent gales that bore, one particular night, a special visitor. A timid knocking croaked at them beneath the cacophony of the storm, so very weak and small that neither the King nor the Queen judged it to be a knocking at all, only the wind. Luckily, the Prince had been passing the front door when the stranger knocked, so opened it.

Drenched in cold rain and shivering on the doorstep of this grand castle was a young woman, beautiful to behold. Her dress pulled and tugged by the lascivious wind, her cheeks and chest red-raw with cold, her shoes overflowing with water, she stood. The Prince had never seen so perfect a creature, and soon he was ushering her into the castle to dry off, thanking the gods that they should send to him an angel on the breeze, for certainly she was all he had been looking for. Once dried and restored to the warm glow of youth that powdered her skin, the young woman looked bashfully at the handsome Prince.

'I come only for shelter, and will be on my way once this storm subsides.' That timid voice! Those terrified eyes! The Prince could not stand to think of his life without the company of this golden chaffinch, whose admiration for him radiated stronger as each second passed. He resolved to marry her, at all costs.

Presenting his find to the sombre Queen, the Prince proudly stood aside while the shaking young woman was examined, only to be stolen away by the Prince, taken to some Western room where he could admire her in clearer light.

'She is pretty, but has she the delicacy of a princess? Will she pass my test?' moaned the Queen to the King, who shrugged, threw the last of his scotch into the window plants and poured himself another to sink the pain from the ulcer in his stomach.

The Prince too was worried about the pea beneath those forty mattresses; for the young woman could never be his if she did not prove her frailty to his mother. To conquer this frustrating difficulty, he professed his love to the young woman and rejoiced in its reciprocation, hesitantly admitted after much blushing and trembling.

'Oh, but I fear we can never be united!' he fretted, placing his head in his hands before glancing up at the young woman, framed in the innocent rays of a lightning bolt. Having not the nerve to ask him why this was so, she waited for the next clap of thunder and focused her eyes on her beloved, sure not to look too intensely, lest he should think her forward. The Prince continued, 'my mother has hidden a pea beneath your mattresses, and if you cannot feel it tonight, as you sleep, she will not allow our marriage.' He pretended to weep in deep, harrowing groans. The young woman steeled herself to speak and opened those sweet lips, pink as dawn-clouds, in preparation—but the Prince interrupted, 'of course, if we show her that the tiny pea has done you great injury by lurking beneath your mattresses, she will hasten to embrace you as her daughter.'

Uncovering his face, the Prince approached his fresh sweetheart with an evil in his eyes that had never before breached the castle's walls, and had, perhaps, swept through on some malignant draught the night of his birth. The eyes of the young woman were suddenly her only mobile organ, for fear had frozen her synapses and broken her spine, aiding the Prince by eliminating the chase he had expected. Soon her nose was broken by his fist, and blood swung like the saliva of a sleeping child from her chin onto the carpet, forevermore. Though she wept and cowered, the Prince dragged the waif up and beat her down again, in that well-lit, dusty chamber in the West of the castle, where screams could only carry themselves so far before getting lost. Over and over, she failed to avoid his ever-raining punches, and suffered in his grip. Soon, when the young woman was barely conscious and broken in several places, the Prince carried her to her chamber and placed her atop the forty mattresses. He kissed her bruised forehead.

'Good night, my princess.' He whispered.

*

The next morning, two servants were sent by the Prince to collect their guest when she did not arrive at breakfast. A half an hour passed and, eventually, in she hobbled, black and blue and bleeding from the mouth, even after passing a night in repose. The Queen, when dragged from her reverie by her elated son, expressed a touching maternal concern for the young woman.

'How came you by these injuries? Why, my dear; you're battered half to death!' But the young woman made no reply, just sobbed silently into her handkerchief and waited for fate to laugh.

'Isn't it obvious, mother?' cried the Prince. 'The pea in the mattress did this! Her skin was punctured by that cruel vegetable. Have you ever seen a princess so deserving of her title?' And, in her unhappy, deluded state, the Queen believed her handsome son, the child who would sire for her several other children, the kind with love in their hearts and light in their souls.

The Prince and the young woman married the next day, and lived in the castle until their deaths. The Princess bore the Prince eight children, each as spiteful and cruel as their father, and spent her life fluttering between utter despondency and hysteria. Every time a storm came, however, she would cry with the strength of an unloved child, for she would remember the penny-sized bruise that the pea had once left at the base of her spine.

There, that is a true story.

Figure 5 Vicious Vegetable

The Witch of Hardknot Pass

Jade Diamond

It is strange to be back near my childhood home of Hardknot Pass after spending so many years away. I crane my neck to look out the window, to try to glimpse some artefact of my former life, but it is too dark to see outside. My young son, Bartholomew, sits opposite, and I notice he is struggling to stay awake. I used to tell him the stories of magic and fairies from my homeland, but my wife thinks that they have been giving him nightmares. Lately, he has been telling her about seeing a headless woman surrounded by dozens of tiny shadows. He tells her she steals children.

I thought it strange when she told me this—it was one of the legends of my childhood, after all, but not one I'd told my son. I wouldn't dare frighten Bartholomew with the story of Mildred Phyllis.

*

Mildred was beautiful, and married to a prosperous farmer. Many of the village women were jealous, and spread rumours about her. There were suggestions that she had attained her beauty by less-than-earthly means, and that she had somehow tricked her husband into marriage. Often joining the townswomen in their talk was the village priest. Everyone knew he lusted after Mildred—though of course, he could not act on it. He blamed Mildred for 'tempting' him, and his bitter resentment flourished over the years. When her husband and child died in the same year, Mildred received a great deal of public sympathy. Privately, the rumours and gossip continued to swirl.

One autumn the crops failed seemingly overnight. Thick, icy frosts settle on the fields, crushing the delicate stalks. In the field behind Mildred's home, cows lay down and died. A number of children fell ill with fits and fever. The villagers were spooked: some said Mildred's grief was so deep that she reached out to dark forces to return her family. And that those dark forces were meddling in our affairs as a sort of repayment.

After a few weeks, the villagers decided they'd had enough. One night, Mildred was dragged from her home and into the village square. Three burly men stood over, forcing her neck onto the chopping block. The priest walked from his church, incense holder swinging, dispersing its sickly-sweet smelling smoke into the crisp night air.

As he approached the block, he passed the thurible to an acolyte, and graciously accepted a pickaxe.

'It is clearly written in the book of Exodus,' he called out to the assembled crowd, 'thou shalt not suffer a witch to live!'

The crowd gently murmured its assent as he drew up the axe and brought it firmly down on her exposed neck.

I was not much older than Bartholomew on that night. Most of what I remember about it is likely fantasy; just bits and pieces that I've picked up each time the story was told and retold during my childhood. What I am certain of, is that she made no sound. She never protested; she never begged for mercy; she never screamed. She was silent.

Mildred was buried in an unmarked grave—the priest said a sinner such as she did not deserve a headstone. As a boy, we'd go to her gravesite and stand by it, just to feel the temperature turn cold. Our mothers said we were foolish for saying her grave had the power to change the weather; but we were warned against going there just the same. A child would not—could not—have read the fear in those maternal eyes.

A few weeks after her burial, the wintry weather worsened. The soil froze, and the nights became longer and colder. High winds came with darkness; doors and windows were ripped from their hinges. Then the children went missing.

*

One by one, every child in the village disappeared. The older children were first—a pair of fourteen year olds. Rumour was that they must have run off to marry, but the next night, and the next, children were found missing from their homes. By the time the babies started disappearing, the villagers were blaming Mildred.

They said that she had come back from the dead, claiming the children as her own. Some of the elders in the village claim to have seen her walking across the top of Hardknot Pass, holding the children's hands as she lead them down the steep paths, never to be seen again. Some have tried to follow her, but they lose her when they walk through the winding paths. I was one of the few that were left. My mother and father left the village to keep me safe after the first spate of disappearances.

The carriage suddenly came to an abrupt halt, interrupting my recollections. The lantern fell to the floor and I crushed the flame beneath my feet before it spread. Bartholomew looked around frantically and his breathing started to quicken.

'Father, what is happening?'

'Stay here. I'll go speak to the coachman.'

'I want to go with you, father!'

'Wait here.' The thought of Mildred ran a shiver down my spine. 'It is not safe outside.'

I stepped outside into the brisk air. A sharp gust of wind wrapped its arms around me and ripped open my coat. As I walked toward the front of the carriage, I realised that both the horse and coachman were gone. I looked over the path into the dimly-lit abyss, but I could see them. Some of the stones beneath my feet came loose and fell into the canyon; I could not hear them hitting the bottom. I had not noticed how close we were to the edge of the precipice. 'Bartholomew,' I called out, 'stay in the carriage. Do not venture out here.'

Slowly and gingerly I make my way back to the carriage. 'Bartholomew, are you well, son? Do not be frightened. The coachman has had to stop for—'

But Bartholomew was gone.

There were scratches covering the seats, and I saw his jacket lying on the floor. I sat down and tried to control my breathing. The wind bellowed and raged outside, rocking the carriage back and forth. Suddenly the doors of the carriage slammed shut. I pushed against them—think it was merely the wind—but the wooden doors would not budge. An ear-piercing screech sounded from just outside the carriage. I drew back the curtain and saw a pale hand dragging its nails across the window. No face. No person. Just the hand.

'Father'!' Bartholomew screamed from outside. I pound the door and pull at the handle but it is for nought. The carriage creaks as it starts to roll. I scream for the coachman, but there is no one driving. Ripping the curtain from the back window, I look out to see her standing there with my son. I pound on the carriage with my fists; I scream and beg for mercy. But she only stands and watches with Bartholomew—my Bartholomew—by her side. She presses his face to her skirts to keep him quiet, but he holds out a small hand to me. They grow smaller and smaller; blurring in my tears.

Mildred is satisfied with her findings tonight.

Figure 6 Spectral Visions

REVERIE

JOSEPH BRASH

Childhood: often perceived as a time of such innocence, an untainted canvas of experience. For many a millennia mankind has longed to remain youthful, yet remain ignorant to the fostering darkness of infancy.

One such boy succeeded, a fairy tale brought to reality, free from the shackles of life imposed upon him by adults. You may have heard of him? Of him and his lost boys? He was their fearless leader, their captain of adventure, their executioner. A truth lurks about him, a truth we choose to ignore about youth: a shrug of the shoulder, the turning of an eye, all towards the inherently egocentric and narcissistic selfishness of immaturity.

Though, it is not he that we focus our attention upon today; instead we are directed to what it is he left behind, the remains of his Wendy. He carved himself into her heart and abandoned her, ensuring the belief that his return remains intact, refusing the delusion that her adventure wasn't fact.

Of course, she isn't left utterly alone; she exists within a peculiar residency, the current occupiers of an aid-giving establishment. Unlike the others, she regularly rekindles solace from the Porter's diurnal surveyance. Daily routines brought about a sense of familiarity to one another, and with that came an unnervingly pleasant warmth of kinship.

Now, Wendy was often found sat by her window, a forlorn sentry incessantly searching for her boy who never grew up.

'Wendy,' the Porter would say, 'you're wasting your life away.' But he could never understand. 'My dear Wendy,' he'd declare, 'I beg of you, turn away from the window for just a second, it'll do you the world of good.' But what world was that? He was not from her world; he had not experienced life as she did.

'I mustn't look away for a second!' she'd remind him. 'If I were to miss him I... I could never forgive myself.'

The Porter grew more accustomed to her each day, taking a step closer into her room upon each visit. The conversations didn't provide much, but the companionship delivered a sustenance both were lacking. His attempts of condolences were unnecessary to Wendy; his caring nature gratified her and in return he found a reason to live. Routines became obsessions, and the burrowing demon of jealousy sunk deeper into the skin of him.

Why does she wait for him? I'm here for her, every day. Yet she still loves him. A chill prickled the hairs upon his arms as he once again entered Wendy's dwelling.

'You're getting too old for this Wendy. You must grow up.' A silent sickness flourished, her head turned, fluid eyes piercing through his heavy soul.

'I can't grow old, I mustn't! He will not return for me otherwise! And I know it, I just know he will.'

'It's not true,' the Porter insisted, 'but I remain here for you.' Her silence replied to him, unrequited emotions speaking through the muteness.

His envy burrowed deeper, from the skin and into his heart, eventually claiming the very bones of his being. The passing weeks of silence created nothing but torment, his conscience was degrading, obsession purveying. '*She needs to know the truth. I need to show her, it's me who she shall love*'.

Red-faced and flushed, he became the specimen of Dutch courage. Jealousy and anger embellished amongst the nocturnal, the early morning mindset that niggles its way into the heads of the hurt. Balancing his face between a thumb and forefinger, his presumptions paced between the plans of how he may proceed, he could not wait. Mutterings of a madman meandered through his mind, a cracked conscience. Embracing the keys to Wendy's cell, he had enough.

Bleary-eyed the Porter set off through streets and corridors; but his state of reverie remained aloft. There he stood panting and gasping for breath, the cold air cutting at his lungs. Wendy's door seemed larger, heavier in stance. He was losing his poise; a fear stuck him, a conscience in combat within its own character.

'Who's there?' Wendy called. 'I can hear you; don't pretend you're not there!' This was his time. A cluttering of keys and a burst through the door, he could see the silhouette of Wendy lingering by the window. 'Porter? What are you—'

'You know what he did. Don't you Wendy?' he said as he slithered closer to her bed. 'I've watched you, Wendy. You're a lost soul, like me. But we could have each other.' Wendy did not budge, her eyes immersed through the window bars of her cell. 'Look at me Wendy! God help me he was a murderer! Why do you remain captivated by him so! Children, Wendy! It was all a game to him, can't you see that!?'

'It wasn't like that,' she answered. 'He warned them, they fully understood the rules of the game. You can never grow up with him.'

'What of the parents Wendy? How do you think they feel, their infants stolen? Children, slaughtered?'

'I was to be their mother, they agreed. It was the only way.'

His heart pounding through his chest, he could barely swallow his breath, aggression eclipsed him, and envy commanded him. Hands clasped around the fullness of her face,

'Just look at me Wendy, look at me! Not at him!' As her eye line met his, darkness filled the room. A swooping shadow bellowed through every crack, the air became thick and congested.

'He's here.'

The Porters shrieks of panic were silenced while the blackness consumed him. He was suffocated by a boy's shadow. His skin crunched, his stature degraded, and youth abandoned him like that of a leper. Wendy finally took notice of the Porter, waiting until his enduring ashes blew away with the wind, the weight of his soul now void.

Wendy returned to her window, the shadow aerating itself towards the gap between the bars, touching her fingertips before finally dispelling itself into the night sky. And there she remained, waiting; ensuring the boy she loved would never grow up. Holding on, keeping faith, solid in the knowledge that it shall be her time soon enough.

She refused to forget, 'second to the right and straight on till morning.'

Figure 7 Hangin' Around

NORTHERN NIGHTMARES

Figure 8 Roarie Battles the Redcaps

ONCE UPON A TYNE

COLIN YOUNGER

Once upon a Tyne it was
Beside that mighty stream
There dwelt a Redcap couple
Held highly in esteem.

They had four sons whom they had raised
To uphold the Redcap code
And though they were quite handsome
They were a little pigeon-toed

Redcaps can be fearsome
Pray never get them mad
They can manifest as Mordred
Instead of Galahad

Their beaks are strong; their talons sharp
To rip and tear scratch
Yet strong in arm and capable
Of adversarial despatch.

The lads were mighty, strong and tough
Ne'er timid in a battle
And just like many around that time
They helped themselves to cattle

Now we must off to Simonside
Across the boggy moor
'Tis hilly country just the place
To find young ladies pure

They have up and gone away
True love they'll find for sure
For each there'll be just one such maid
Residing with the poor

Across the moors and through the dales
Full speedily they rode
Not sparing nags they reached the place
Where Duergars find abode

As they pulled up they heard a rustle
From in the copse entwined
When from the trees there stepped a man
With large head and behind.

Say who ye be ye scurvy knave
Young Radgie did demand
I'm Roarie King of Simonside
Kneel down and kiss my hand.

Figure 9 Gadgie

'We'll no such thing ye great poltroon'
Yelled Gowk at this intruder
'I'll skelp your hide you hairy ape'
The rest was somewhat cruder

Now Duergar are unpleasant beasts
They're proud of being so
They'd sooner rip a gizzard out
And maul the bits below

And now they're up and scrapping hard
To see who is the strongest
They're quite well matched these Northern sorts
It's really who lasts longest!

The Redcap boys all four are up
Full riving at the Creature
Who battles hard against his foe
'Til gore becomes a feature.

For hours they're fighting tooth and claw
No wish to taste dishonour
Ne'er a thought of yielding though
They might well be a goner?

Then all at once appears a sight
That no-one will forget
It's Roarie's Ma with broom in hand
Most scary thing seen yet!

Now pack it in Just stop right now
Ye wild young ragamuffin
I'll set about ye so I will
Ye'll know ye've had a duffin'

Figure 10 Radgie Revisited

The Redcap lads now stand up small
And thrust their chests before them
Young Roarie he skulks back red-faced
Now no Victor Ludorum.

We're not afraid of Duergar folk
We'll not be following you
Or else we'll fall right to our doom
And we'll be forced to sue.

Young Gowk was not a clever lad
But he knew the tales his Ma
Had told him as a weenie child
Supported by his Da.
Heid (his Da) had courted long
His Ma by name of Hinny
He really loved his Redcap wife
Particularly her pinny.

When they first met they contemplated

Running off together
But love was stopped still in its tracks
By far too clement weather

Some talked of women beauteous
Such as The Flower of Yarrow
With perfect features, pouting lips
And waist impossibly narrow.

But Hinny was a different beast
Heid's perfect Redcap bride
With curling nails and razor teeth
The Weed of Simonside.

But Roarie's Ma is here right now
Stinking, fat and gruesome
With her huge offspring growling low
A terrifying twosome.

She lifts a lantern to her face
And beckons them come thither
As many times she's done before
And ta'en travellers with her.

The Redcap boys are wise to this
And tell the dreadful hag
That they will not be lured away
Which makes her jowls sag

A tryst is set and all decide
To go to Deurgar land
So ride they do most speedily
This strange and ghastly band.

And they've arrived and set up camp
Right by the Duergars' side
The Redcaps now so rightly keen
To find themselves a bride.

A feast is called and merriment
The order of the day
They'll roast the lonely traveller
Who next should chance their way.

With fire lit and rover skewered
The Duergar are all set
Redcap feathers bristling
Their appetites are whet.

And as they're up and whirling wild
The Duergar girls select
The Redcap boys who seem to speak
Their own sub-dialect.

Gadgie looks around the females there
And wraps his eyes round Grot
Her slimy skin and oily hair
With yearning he's besot

And Gowk is up and dancing slow
With a lass who's known as Hackie
Her ingrown toenails turn him on
And he becomes her lackey.

Young Howk has now become engrossed
With fledgling young Miss Grubby
Her runny nose and scruffy face
Enticing her new hubby.

But Radgie will have none of it
For in amongst the laughter
With no Goodbyes he's leaving them
Living happily ever after.
                    To be continued …

DRAGON

MICHELLE MCCABE

'Nana, will you tell me that story again?'

'Which one, pet?' Grace folded the newspaper and placed it on the floor. She didn't want Joe seeing the front page—another local child abducted from his bedroom.

'The one about the worm!'

'Alright, Joe, and then it's straight to bed. Your mam'll kill me if she finds out I've let you stay up this late.' She always gave in to her only grandchild.

She sat Joe on her knee, shut her eyes, and recited, from memory, the story of the Lambton Worm. His eyes lit up as she spoke of the ancient monster and the brave knight sent to vanquish him. As ever, Joe grinned broadly at the end. Grace smiled down at her young charge.

'My, Joe, what geet big teeth you have. I bet you've got some of the Worm's blood inside you!' she teased.

'Aw, Nana. You said that the last time too. Na-night.'

'Na-night, love.'

She watched Joe climb the stairs. He seemed to be growing taller every day. When she heard his bedroom door snap shut, she rose, turned out the lamp and followed him up, eager to have a bath, and soak her tired bones.

*

Grace awoke in darkness. There was a dull pain at the base of her neck where she'd fallen asleep at a strange angle. The candles were now burned down to smouldering stubs, and the bath water was freezing. She shivered as she stood and reached for the towel that had been resting on the radiator. The warmth of the fabric soothed her only until she opened the door to the hall. She felt an icy-cold wind blowing through the house.

Could I have left a window open? she thought for a moment, before remembering that day's headlines.

'Joe!' she called out, as she raced to his door. 'Joe! Joe!'

She pushed open the door to his bedroom, and watched as his dinosaur-printed curtain flapped in the cold night air above the empty bed.

'Emergency; which service please?'

'Police! Please I need the police! My grandson, he's-he's disappeared from his room.'

'May I take your name and address?'

'Grace Charlton. It's 47 Worm Terrace, Fatfield!'

Grace went downstairs after speaking to the police and reached for the bottle of brandy she kept for emergencies. With a shaking hand, she decanted a rather large glass, and downed it in one.

Her mind raced with the nastiest, foulest possibilities. Where had Joe gone? Who had taken him? And why? Why her darling Joe?

Grace was not a religious woman, but at that moment felt an urge to pray. *Please*, she whispered, *please let my boy be safe.*

A brisk knock interrupted her thought. She put the glass down on the table and tried to compose herself on the short walk to the front door. She lifted the latch and was met by a man and woman, both in suits.

The man had a military bearing; he was well over six feet tall, trim, with a salt-and-pepper hair. The woman looked as tired as her crumpled suit. The man offered his identity card. 'Mrs Charlton?' he asked.

Graced nodded.

'I'm DCI Frank Jefferson.' He nodded toward his colleague, 'my sergeant, Denise Tyler.'

'Come in.'

'Thank you, Mrs Charlton. We know this is difficult for you, but we must ask you some questions.'

Grace nodded as she shut the door behind them.

'Your grandson was taken from his room; is that correct?' asked Jefferson.

'Yes. I don't—I didn't…'

Jefferson held up hand. 'The bedroom is upstairs, Mrs Charlton?'

'It is. I'll show you.' Grace started up the stairs and the detectives followed. She reached Joe's room and paused. 'The 999 operator told me not to go in.'

'It's okay, Mrs Charlton,' said Tyler as she pulled on a pair of gloves. 'We can take it from here.'

Grace stood in the doorway and watched as Jefferson started photographing Joe's room. She heard Tyler mutter, 'we've got a trail, Frank.' For the first time, Grace noticed the floor. A shiny, slimy trail crossed the room, from window to bed. It looked like a slug trail, but it was two feet wide. Grace shuddered at the thought of a slug capable of making a trail that size.

Jefferson noticed Grace looking at the trail. He cleared his throat. 'We will just be a few minutes, Mrs Charlton, if you'd like to go back downstairs and make yourself comfortable.'

Grace started to ask if they'd like a cuppa, but Tyler shut the door in her face.

*

Clutching a steaming mug of tea, Grace sat on the edge of the sofa seat, waiting for the detectives to question her. *They recognised the trail*, she thought. *That's a good sign, surely; must mean they have some clues as to who did this.*

Grace heard Joe's door open, and Tyler soon appeared at the top of the stairs. Grace stood as she watched the young woman make her way down.

'Have a seat, Mrs Charlton. I'd just like to ask you a few questions about the events of this evening.'

Grace resumed her seat. 'What do you need to know?'

'What time did Joe go to bed?' Tyler asked, a she flipped open a notepad.

'Half nine. It's later than he's usually allowed but I was telling him a story. The story of the Worm—the Lambton Worm. It's his favourite so I thought it would be okay just this once, even though it's a school night.' Grace knew she was babbling, but she couldn't stop the words coursing forth. 'He's such a good boy, our Joe. A bonny lad. He just—he loves his fairy stories and it's... it's his favourite,' she repeated, pathetically.

'What time did you go to bed tonight, Mrs Charlton?'

'Well, I didn't. I fell asleep in the bath.'

'I see. What happened when you woke in the bath, then?'

'It was cold. Too cold. I thought a window must've been left opened so I went to check on our Joe. And that's when I saw he was... well, he wasn't...'

'Did you notice anything unusual in Joe's room, Mrs Charlton?'

Grace thought for a moment. 'No. Nothing. I mean, the window was open, but that was it. I didn't look around. Should I have? Would that have helped?'

'No, Mrs Charlton. You've done fine.'

Upstairs Joe's door opened and shut swiftly. Tyler stood.

'My colleague has finished, now. We ask that you do not go into Joe's room until we've completely cleared it.'

Jefferson joined them in the sitting room. 'Is everything satisfactory, Tyler?'

'Yes. Mrs Charlton has done very well.'

'Good.' He turned to Grace. 'It's important that you keep out of Joe's room until we have cleared it.'

'Yes; your sergeant's just said.'

'We'll see ourselves out. Thank you for your cooperation, Mrs Charlton.'

Grace nodded and forced a wan smile. As she locked the door behind the detectives, it occurred to her that she'd no idea what she'd say to Joe's mam.

*

Jefferson slammed the car door shut. 'Ring Carlson.'

'Doing it now.'

'I told him this was damn fool idea. *Natural habitat*,' he said bitterly. 'Who gives a good goddamn about its *natural habitat*?'

Tyler rolled her eyes. She'd heard this rant at every incident this month. 'Carlson's not answering his phone. He's probably still in the lab.'

'Worrying about something else's *habitat* probably.'

'He says it's part of our duty of care, Frank.'

'Our duty of care should be to people. Real people; human people!'

'It would've been quick, said Tyler softly. 'Dragon doesn't let them linger, you know.'

'I know, I know. But I still stay we should've re-homed him nearer HMP Durham. Let him feast there!'

Tyler shrugged. 'Carlson says he's more comfortable near this part of the Wear.'

'Yeah, yeah. *Habitat*.'

*

Jefferson parked the car next to the hill.

'I'm just saying, these are bairns. We've all got to eat, but why has it got to be bairns?'

'No idea, Frank.'

There was a rumble as the overgrowth which concealed the entrance to their HQ started to slide apart.

'Bairns,' Jefferson muttered as he shifted gears and let the car roll forward. They both waved at Davy, the security guard, once inside the bunker.

'There's Carlson now' said Tyler. 'Looks like he's running.'

'For the first time in his bloody life.'

'You know,' said Tyler as she opened the car door, 'he *is* our boss.'

'And he doesn't half love reminding us of it, does he?'

Tyler shut the door behind her. Best to let Frank cool off for a few minutes.

'Were any remains found?' she asked Carlson, as he reached their car.

'No, nothing. He's fond of swallowing whole these days. It'll be the ageing—can't chew as well anymore.'

'There was a trail in the victim's room. Pretty small, but his grandmother saw it.'

'Did she ask about it?'

'No. Her primary concern was the vic.'

'Don't call him a victim!' shouted Frank as he exited the car. 'Call him the boy. Or Joe.' He punctuated this rebuke with a slam of the car door.

'I see your mood has not improved, Frank.'

'No, Carlson. It hasn't. I'm sick of you indoor types and your namby-pamby attitudes toward these creatures! In my day we kept them locked up. We kept people safe.'

'Happily, it's no longer *your day*, Frank,' said Carlson, reddening slightly. 'They have rights, you know. The right to live and to feed. They were here before us and they'll be here long after us!'

'What about the rights of the children he's eating!'

Tyler stepped in between her colleagues.

'Can we focus on the matter at hand, please? Carlson, has the team safely secured Dragon for the night?'

'Yes. Although I think we all know how I feel about those cages.'

Tyler ignored his commentary. 'Frank, you and I will go back to the grandmother's house tomorrow to do damage control. She still thinks we're with the police, after all.'

'Right.'

'Yes, yes; very good,' said Carlson, reaffirming his position as head of the agency. 'Frank, I'd like your report on my desk tomorrow by five o'clock.'

A loud screech from somewhere below them drowned out Frank's reply.

It was hungry again.

Figure 11 Lambton Worm

It loves its natural habitat. It loves the freedom to travel along the banks of the River Wear; feeling the cool night air on its scales. It loves the hunt; it had missed it, after spending so many years locked away. There was no fun in simply being thrown your food, even if the food was screaming and begging for its life. It throws back its head and bellows. It is hungry again.

NOT SO SNOW WHITE

Figure 12 Five Dwarves

CHOKE

SOPHIE RAINE

The knife glided through, piercing the blood red skin and delved into the core, the juice spilling over and pooling on the kitchen worktop. She stared out of the window, continuing to slice the apples; the woodlands appeared so different now that she looked upon them with older, wiser eyes. The young girl in the woods all those years ago did not seem so much like a memory than a tumultuous, aberrant dream from a lifetime ago.

Her father had died when she had been a young girl; she had remembered, with aching nostalgia, the folkloric tales he read to her. It had been he who had named her Eirwen for her alabaster skin that made her look like a china doll against her coarse black hair. She recalled him being the fount of wisdom in her youth; he would know all the answers from what lay on the other side of the forest to why the wolves howl at the moon.

The passing of this man that she had known and loved was only worsened by her mother's immediate remarriage to a man neither of them had particularly known nor wished to get to know. Their wedding had been a tragically, perfunctory affair with a handful of relatives from each side; the look shared between the two newly-weds was not one of love and excitement, but of disappointment and blame.

Her mother had spent her wedding night locked away in her room, sobbing into her wedding dress as her husband drunkenly danced around the garden tripping over his own jacket and shoes which were strewn across the lawn, pitying himself for the wine red bruise that swelled under his eye, which had been given to him by one of the guests who opted for an early departure.

He woke up the next morning, his face and clothes covered in grass stains and lying on his side, courtesy of the maid who was worried he that may choke on his own vomit. Her stepfather's indiscretions seeped through the house like an airborne disease and infected everyone he came into contact with; it was impossible to move around when he was in the vicinity without encountering the misery he had filled it with. His drunken stupors became darkened, violent storms that decimated everything in his path, especially targeting those who had become the focuses of his displeasure, namely his newly found wife and daughter. Over time, Eirwen witnessed his vices crawl to the surface and exposed him as not only a drunk but also a habitual liar and prolific gambler. The incident that drove her from his paternal care and into the blustering cold winds and rain of the night, started with the small, modest collection of jewellery her father had given to her when she was younger. They weren't worth much to the realm of commerce but to a young girl it was a treasure trove, and to a young women they were the signifiers of her father's unyielding love and affection should she need to recall it when memory failed her. Her stepfather had procured a bounteous amount of debt and, realising he was in too deep and fearing for his safety, sold her treasure trove for a pitiful amount to keep the usurers at a safe distance for a little longer. On discovering this, she confronted her stepfather to find his apologies worn, tiresome and saturated in apathy.

Distraught from their encounter she ran into the woodlands as the skies flooded with ink and the heavens opened; the rain pasted her clothes to her skin and knotted her obsidian black tresses into fine wired tendrils that blustered behind her in the winds, desperately wrapping themselves around wizened tree branches and tearing themselves free from her scalp. The broken bark that carpeted the ground splintered under her weight and cut into her feet as she stumbled in the dark. The woodlands burst alive with a myriad of noises that screamed and howled, their echoes bouncing off the trees; she dragged herself to the edge of the forest where the mud turned to grass. The moonlight cast a shadow over the man who stood at the edge of the forest, he was weather-beaten and wild, his axe anchored to the ground. Paralysed by cold and fear, she sat at the edge of the woods unable to move as the sounds blurred, the ground shook, darkness filled and she collapsed to the floor.

She woke later that evening to the screech of the steaming kettle on the stove and looked around to see the woodsman snatching it from the hearth and shrugging at her apologetically. She had been wrapped in a large tartan quilt and placed in front of the crackling hearth, her feet dressed in muslin cloth bandages. Placing the mug in her cupped hands, he took a seat in the armchair next to her, uncomfortably fidgeting with the frayed fabrics on the chair. He seemed gentler in the light, the edges of his face even appeared softer and his presence was not as intruding as when she first encountered him in the midst of the storm. He spoke quietly and sporadically, tiptoeing around her like an unwanted guest in his own home as he strained, with great effort, to muffle any noise he made, deafeningly aware of his own presence. The quiet hung between them in a sober and tranquil manner, it allowed time for them to gather their thoughts. It waited patiently for one of them to begin.

They stayed up throughout the night as she explained why she was out so late and in such weather. He remained quiet while she talked, allowing her story to fill the vacuum in his home where there had been silence for so long. When she had finished, he informed her that, providing she contributed to the workload as best she could, she was invited stay there as long as it pleased her to do so. The woodsman owned the mine next to the orchid where a handful of young boys worked for him. He told her of how living here had been profitable but isolated and that any company was appreciated. Weeks grew into months and months into years, over which time she had become not only his tenant and friend but also his wife.

She lay in their bed each night with her head pressed to his chest listening to his breathing as they intertwined their fingers together and even though he was still as reticent as when they first met, she loved him all the same. He was not simply a facet of her new life, he was her new life; the pillar of safety that protected her from what lay on the other side of the woods and guarded her from the hand that would reach out and drag her back to her harrowing past.

Then came the sleepless nights that opened doors in their untarnished, new lives—doors which should have remained closed. The woodsman had woken abruptly in a hot sweat, his heart frantically trying to break through his ribs. She had remembered how she had felt that night he found her, how he had comforted her even though, initially, he did not understand. Eirwen pushed his damp stray hairs from his face and waited for him to explain why he had awoken such a state for the third night now. He calmed down and began to tell her about when he was a young man, back when he had just acquired trade with merchants over precious metals found in the mine on his property near the orchid. He had gone for a walk one morning and crossed paths with an elderly woman; he recognised her as a traveller whose clan was living in a part of the woods not far from where they were standing. For a small price she said she would tell him his fortune, knowing that there were those who lived in the woods whose visions were almost always true, he gave the woman some coin and listened as she warned him of his fate. 'You will not rest easy while you live at the orchid. A young boy is to be watched out for, he will take your money and your mantle before he takes your life'.

He told her of how he had never slept easy living here and of the watchful eye he kept over all the boys who worked at the mine for fear that those who steal from him would attempt to murder him. Eirwen's father had always told her that fortune telling was a way for peddlers to make money and never held any credence in his eyes so her worries mostly focused on her husband and whether his kind, benevolent demeanour would slip into an erratic, impulsive nature should his paranoia continue.

The sunlight poured down the next morning like honey and blanketed over their land giving everything an amaranthine glow. The boys shielded their eyes from the sun's unwanted rays with their bony, muddied arms. She hadn't realised how small the boys were until their shapes were cast on the ground like shadow puppets revealing their formless, willowy frames. Now she observed them with more scrutiny she looked beyond their gaunt faces to their sunken, docile eyes which judged and shamed. They were the kind of dead eyes that haunt. She tore her gaze away from them, plucking one of the ripened apples from the tree, shining it with her sleeve. Her husband shouted from a few yards away and briskly jogged towards her taking it from her, he looked relieved and smiled. 'You shouldn't eat what grows in the orchid,' he warned, smiling warmly as he planted a tender kiss on her forehead.

Eirwen started to retreat to the cottage then took another look back around at her husband. She saw the woodsman talking to one of the boys; he put his knife towards the boy holding out a piece of apple on the blade. She couldn't make out the words on the woodsman's lips but watched as the boy began to cough, spluttering and grasping at his throat. The woodsman stood over the boy as he turned puce, watching with a smug sanctimony as his small body dropped to the floor. Then the coughing stopped. The only sound to be heard was the circling crows up ahead looking with avarice at their new carrion.

The funeral was a rushed affair; there were no speeches or outbursts of grief, just a sea of terrified boys' faces and the sound of dirt hitting the wood of the coffin. No words were exchanged as they went to bed that night; they turned away as they undressed, as if they were strangers. She dwelled on what he had told her a few nights prior and wondered if this madness would end now. Had he caught his usurper? Was he lying in the ground in a custom made coffin with a piece of apple caught in his throat? Her father once told her of the barbaric nature of those who live beyond the woods, how they live to survive because of the harsh conditions. Merchants and tradesmen were known to kill those under their wing if they believed they had stolen from them, and it was common knowledge that the deceased boy had, along with many of them, stolen. If it was a fear of being robbed then she could sleep easy knowing that the boys had been deterred and it was unlikely to happen again, yet she could not settle that night with worry that this was not why the woodsman had killed the boy. If his laws were meted out based on apparitions in dreams and fraudulent fortune tellers then he may never be sated, he may never sleep right which meant that they, the boys and herself, would never sleep right either.

One night, her husband sat behind her wrapping his arms around her body, feeling his way down he felt down, underneath her breasts, to the protruding dome which held their child. He circled his hands around the sphere of the bump kissing her neck; she smiled with him, fat with love for them both. With parenthood, loomed the promise of change and their sleepless nights will be of dutiful care and not waking from the panicked abrupt awakening of her husband. As he looked enamoured at her stomach, she felt that fatherhood would bring with it sense and reason that had previously eluded him, these ideas of murder and betrayal will seem like the delusions of a madman that he will recall with remorse and embarrassment. The young boys in the mine would no longer fear him, no longer would they have to carve coffins and wonder who would be occupying them. He would fall, surely, in love with his child and the rest of the world would fall away and be no longer of interest. For a few nights after discovering she was with child, his suspicion was banished from his dreams and the woodsman knew peace once more.

As time passed, while she did not hear him awaken from his sleep, she noticed the tired, worn expression on his face. He would shrink away from her when she attempted to touch his face, to bring him back to their world. She became not the object of his affection but something to be feared.

He would often spend his nights in front of the fire downstairs resisting sleep. On several occasions, Eirwen would try to place his hands on her stomach to feel their baby but he always pulled his hand away sharply as if deeply terrified of what was growing inside her womb. When she spoke, he looked at her but the glassy expression in his eyes betrayed that he had not even recognised she was there. It killed her, watching him slip into an abyss where she could not follow but knowing something of the dark thoughts he held. She had tried to convince herself that he may be in ill health, and that he may have some worries about fatherhood but ultimately she knew that his reservations came from that same fear that woke him from his sleep for years. He stared at her stomach the same way he would stare at the boys in the mine, the same way he looked at the boy from the orchid that day. It had been easier to console herself to the idea that he was a changed man, that his entire adult life had been stifled by morbid delusions that he was ready to accept weren't true. What he had been told, those many years ago, had gnawed at every aspect of his goodness and his sanity, only leaving behind a taciturn and suspicious figure in its wake. *Something must be done*, she reconciled.

Eirwen placed the freshly cut apples she had gathered that morning, into the pastry lined dish ready for her husband to come home. She delicately folded over the top layer of the pie with care and attention to detail, as though it would somehow make it right. After placing it in the oven, she sat down at the table and waited for his return.

When he arrived home, she placed his food in front of him, the crockery rattling in her hands. Staring questioningly at the dish placed in front of him, the woodsman turned to her. He noted the way that her hands shook and her eyes darted to avoid him, that awkward fidgeting in her seat desperate to break free. 'You're not eating?' He asked her.

She smiled and explained she had been feeling nauseous. He turned to the young boy cleaning the benches and demanded:

'You. Try this.' He crouched closer to him placing the food on the fork near to his mouth like an infant. 'Go on,' he urged.

He gave one last sly smile to his wife before feeding the forkful of food to the boy. She ran over to him and grabbed his cheeks forcing him to spit out the half-chewed food as he coughed and spluttered on the floor; she ushered him out the house and kept a safe distance from the woodsman. He picked up the plate examining the pie from every angle, half-amused with madness. 'Do you think me stupid?'

Words choked her; they crawled up her throat and died there leaving her nothing but pained signs that pleaded for him to understand, to see what he had become. He picked up the stein from the table and hurled it across the room, she dodged its path but the remnants of glass shattered off the wall and showered her in tiny cuts.

'Don't you understand?' he screamed moving towards her and grabbing hold of her hair. 'He will kill me!' He flung her to the floor, in front of the fiery hearth, laughing to himself. .It was always the child. You came here all these years ago, out of the woods, fated to bring me to my death!'

She stretched her arms out feeling for the metal rod of the fire iron.

'The son born to kill the father.'

He stooped to the floor crawling closer to her, she could feel his warm breath on the back of her neck as she inched closer to the hearth. She screamed, plunging her hands into the flames and grabbed the fire iron as it burnt and blistered in the palm of her hands; she heaved it upwards and struck down the woodsman. Then there was silence, for a moment. She dropped the burning metal and screamed, falling down exhausted into a heap on her husband, feeling his beating heart and his slowing breath.

The boys gathered around outside the orchid, silent around him waiting for her as she trudged over. Eirwen moved over to the boys and cast her eyes on their handiwork, weeks in the making and it was sublime. A small, aching smile crept on her face for a second. She stared down at the glass coffin, moving her fingers around the sharp edges and looking at him as he peacefully slept. It was bigger than she had imagined when she asked the boys to craft it for her many moons ago, she hadn't realised how frail he had become from not eating or sleeping. His eyes snapped open and stared up at his wife as he placed his hand onto the top of the glass. She looked away for a moment, blinking back burning tears that stung in her eyes when she saw the look of confusion and desperation on his face. Frozen for a moment, she took her chance to speak.

Eirwen told him of how she loved him but that her child will not be another victim of his madness. She jumped slightly as he hit the roof of the coffin sending a reverberation through the glass. He looked pitiful lying there slamming his hands against the walls of his cell, his screams were muffled and his hands were starting to bruise. She planted a kiss on the top of the glass leaving a blood red stain behind her. The woodsman, though he did not at first understand, quickly learned what it was like to choke.

Figure 13 ... The Other Two

An Overturned Tale

Emily Bird

The glow along the horizon grew like a wave upon the sand; the sky was streaked with burning oranges and delicate pinks. The shadows of night shrank as I watched the sun rise over the fields before the castle. My mind was delighted at such beauty. If only I could be as beautiful as a sunrise.

'Magic mirror in my hand; who is fairest in the land?'

'My queen, you are fairest in the land.'

I smiled at its reply. Setting the magic mirror back into my locked drawer, I glanced back out of the window at the sunrise.

'Mother, can you hear that?' I whispered. 'I am fairest in the land.'

I was sure that my whispers stretched as far as the seas beyond the horizon. All I could remember of my mother was her hatred for me. She never approved of anything that I did; she was only ever concerned with my looks: 'tie your hair up to put waves in it!'; 'pinch your cheeks to add some colour'; 'sleep for long hours to ensure your beauty rest.'

Now I was beautiful: golden curls delicately sat on my bare shoulders, a glow emanated from my sun-kissed skin, and my eyes dazzled like the stars that twinkle on the edge of a twilight sky.

I heard a short, sharp knock at the door. 'Come in,' I called.

'The king requests your presence, ma'am,' said the servant, grimly.

I heaved a heavy sigh; reluctant to depart from my daydreams. Shoulders slumped, I walked down the dimly-lit corridor to the chamber of the king—my husband.

'My darling,' he called out weakly. I crossed to his bedsides and grasped his white, withered hand. 'Promise me,' he said, his voice shaking, 'promise me that you'll look after Snow White.'

I leaned down to kiss my dying husband's papery cheek. 'My love, I shall do as you wish.'

'Then I may depart the world a happy man.' His voice seemed to fade as rapidly as the light in his eyes.

Tears burned in my eyes, and ran down my cheeks. 'I will always love you,' I whispered.

His hand went limp, and my shock at its heaviness caused me to drop it onto the bed. With a harsh rattle, his last breath escaped his body. I trembled with fear and heartbreak, as I wept for my lost love. The only person who had made me feel beautiful was gone. The only person who had truly loved *me* was departed forever.

'Father?'

'No, darling! Don't come in!' I shouted. I wanted to keep Snow White from seeing her father, but it was too late.

Her eyes narrowed in fury and she pointed at me with one shaking hand. 'You did this! You killed him! You poisoned him!'

'Snow White, please! I loved your father more than anything in this world! I wanted to live and long and happy life with him!' But my pleading did nothing to change her mind.

'I will make you pay,' she solemnly vowed before storming away.

I slumped to the ground beside my king's bed. I could not win a war against Snow White without my beloved. How could I protect Snow White if she hated me?

*

Years passed under dreary spells and misfortunes. Days slugged by as the rain pelted to the ground, each rain drop splashing the earth with misery and despair. Snow White had refused to see me. It was hopeless. I wandered the dark castle lost in a haze of nightmares.

I couldn't bear to hold my mirror again. My want for looking for beautiful had passed with my beloved king. The light in my heart had faded like sunlight before a winter's night.

One day, as I watched the rain falling from my window, I heard a gentle knock.

'Enter,' I called, thinking it was a servant. Instead I was greeted by a vision of grace and splendour. Snow White stood before me. She had aged well, and was as striking as her father had been; skin as white as snow, lips as red as blood, and hair as black as a raven.

'Oh, Snow White, have you come to forgive me at last?'

She carried a basket of food in her arms. 'I wanted to apologise for the way that I have treated you over the years. I am ashamed to admit it, but you are beautiful and I was jealous of that.'

'Nothing matters more than our kinship,' I reassured her. 'I have always wanted to love you and protect you; to treat you as though you were my own daughter.'

She smiled. 'I brought you an apology gift. I want to make sure that you know how much you mean to me now. We're all that we have left. We're family.' She stepped towards me, closing the door behind her.

I grasped her shoulder in delight. 'You mean the world to me, Snow White.'

'Here,' she held the basket before me to look inside: cold meats pulled into tender chunks that sat upon a soft bedding of loafs, potatoes that were stewed to perfection under a seasoning of butter and herbs, and apples that shone so brightly that I could see my reflection.

'They look so delightful. And I have nothing for you my dearest! But I shall send my ladies into town tomorrow and they will buy you all the finery you would like!'

Snow White's lips twitched, 'That is not necessary. After all, it is I who is here to humble myself in front of you. Now please; try an apple.'

I lifted a perfectly-formed red orb to my lips, and tasted the wonderful sweet tang of juice dancing on my tongue.

A smile slowly spread across Snow White's face. But it wasn't happiness in her eyes. It was something else...

A burning pain erupted in my stomach, and I collapsed to the floor in a seizing fit. My hot blood scorched my body as my heart beat violently in my chest. Tears blurred my vision as Snow White stood and walked to my locked drawer. She picked up the key before unlocking and opening it to victoriously pick up my magic mirror. I gasped in pain, trying to speak.

'I decided to take action once and for all,' she said coldly. 'You took my father away from me, and so I decided to take your beauty away from you. You poisoned my father's mind with your beauty! I have now taken that away from you.' She smirked down at me. 'An eye for an eye, *stepmother dearest.*'

Bile rose in my throat, bitter and fast. My body shook as the poison spread; I felt its fire everywhere. Blackness started to sweep in along the edges of my vision. I watched, helpless, as my entire world faded into night.

A voice rang out in darkness.

'Magic mirror in my hand; who is fairest in the land?'

'You are, Snow White.'

I will never be the sunrise.

Figure 14 Necronomicon

Of Giants and Trolls

Figure 15 The Huldrefolk

THE HULDREFOLK

ALISON YOUNGER

She'd been born, once upon a time, in her grandmother's cottage while the snow laid siege to the shuddering walls and windows. While the women attended to the mother, he had wrapped her in a blanket and laid her in a suitcase, as the crib they had prepared seemed too big for her tiny body. He named her 'Alice' for his love, and 'Solveig' for his homeland and she grew, black-haired, big-eyed and pale-skinned in his weather-beaten, sea-scented, golden aura where darkness had no influence. When she walked, it was to him, and when she spoke, her first word was his name. In his strange, sonorous accent he called her 'Litten Dukke', 'Little Doll' and sang to her of how the Fenris Wolf can dupe the innocent by inviting her to pick flowers in the forest. And, when he died, the light went out of her world, and, so, she had decided to undertake a quest to the land of the midnight sun; a journey inward to find solace in the world of 'once upon a time'…

The aunts said the heart attack was due to rheumatics. 'Three weeks on a raft when his ship went down in the Atlantic' had weakened him, they said. Their words floated, half-acknowledged in her agonised mind, clouded by a miasma of uncomprehending grief. All that mattered was going back. She'd find him again, she knew, in the Trondelag, where the sun shone at midnight and the sky shone with the lustre of beaten gold set with rubies, emeralds, sapphires and diamonds; where the merry dancers whistled and cracked across the top of the endless towering forests and the *Huldrefolk* crouched, hidden in the narrow and dangerous regions below.

Fittingly, in memory of the seafarer he had been she had taken a boat, a huge cruise-liner, reduced to a child's toy in the towering landscape. As it carved its way through the supremely still, bottomless darkness of the fjords her adult mind mused on the sublimity of the yawning void below, and the limitless expanse of the gothic vistas which stretched their ancient arms, pitted with precariously perched mountain farms around this vast and lovely land of watery shadows. As she stared into the briny abyss, the half-terrified child within her willed the monster-*Draugen* to erupt screaming from his watery grave and drag her, boat and all into the vertiginous depths from which he'd seen legions of Jack-booted, swastika-strewn monsters emerge to take their homes and their homeland as the storms of war gathered in the North Country.

[51]

'There are worse things than ghosts, Litten Dukke', he had said, and she knew that he had seen battleground horrors she could never, and should never imagine.

But how she desired to fathom the fathomless depths beneath her. To an imagination made fragile and evasive by an understanding of the world, it would be a truth of sorts. But the inscrutable waters remained impassive and returned nothing but a spectral veil of clouds looming over the sinister and superlative face of an ageless, elemental mountain, bearded with an impossibly dense and dark forest. No vengeful ghost stretched out his seaweed clad arms. The fjord was not ready to disgorge its secrets yet. So the adult quieted the child with her uncanny imaginings, and focused, with eyes dulled by habit and custom, on the practicalities of her journey into the known unknown, to the scenes and events which had marked her existence and seeped into her sleeping and waking dreams.

'Are you here for the Northern Lights? They say they are beautiful' The enthusiastic, American accent roused her from her reverie.

'In a way' she said, 'I am'.

And in a way she was.

She vaguely heard his snatches of text-book science about polar winds, gas molecules and 'electrically charged particles'.

'Always been on my bucket list' he smiled.

'Mine too' she disingenuously conceded, and, realising that she had no further use for conversation, he walked away, throwing 'have a good trip' over his warmly wrapped shoulder.

'I will' she mouthed, and 'you too', but he was already too far away to hear her insincere platitudes.

Unwilling to tolerate further company she made her way down through the labyrinthine corridors to her cabin and lulled by the imperceptible rocking of the boat and the breath of northern mountains, she slept. In her lucid dreams the child-within-her arrived for the first time at Bestemor's house, clutching the hand of the man who has her father in everything but biology. Enraptured by the blue eyed, broad-boned 'cousins' to whom she bore no genetic relationship, the child, as dark as they were fair crept into herself and further into the books which she carried as talismans to shield her from the world. In her imagination these children; these strange, lithe creatures who could swim like seals and run like the wind, were supernatural creatures who could appear and disappear at will in the uncultivated and uncorrupted landscape, blown by solar winds and illuminated by aurora borealis. Here they sported in the deepest fjords and darkest woods, leaping out of the narrow troughs carved by glaciers; racing along the shingle beaches, that were hugged by precipitous mountain and great snow banks carved into fearfully spiral shapes by an unseen hand. Theirs was a fantasy world of fairy tale geographies – beautiful, grim, savage and dread; a timeless landscape where the laws of nature and the march of ages seemed to be suspended.

Here, where the Trøndelag gives way to the ever wilder and more forbidding province of Nordland, the child arrived, again for the first time at the sacred space of love and loss that was Bestemor's house, a realm of becoming: humble, hospitable and perfect in its fairy tale imperfection. But outside she recalled the stunted pines carved into grotesque monsters and things turned to stone because of the nature of their hearts, and, again she sensed rushing feet, and eyes peering out of the undergrowth as unseen things emerged from the defiled shadows of the World Below.

'There is nothing to fear', she consoled herself; 'during the hours of sunlight they must stay in their underground homes'.

The woman was jolted awake by an insistent knocking on her cabin door. 'Surely not the American' she hoped. Thankfully not. Instead a tinny disembodied accent, rapid and familiar, with the same quaint inflections as his told her that 'passengers should prepare to disembark. We hope you have enjoyed your trip'. Barely awake and haunted by the shades that had stalked her dreams she registered that her trip had not yet started and nor would it until she left the ship behind.

Would she go to Nordland? She didn't know, but grimly determined to complete her pilgrimage to wherever it was she was going, she headed up to the café and picked at the breakfast *smorgasbord*.

'You again'. Her insistent American 'friend', this time in a Norwegian cardigan, plonked himself at the table beside her.

'First time in Trondheim'?

'No' she said, 'I have been here many times' and, shamed by her churlishness of yesterday, she told him of its history, but nothing of hers. Something about him unsettled her, but she pushed the thought away, putting it down to the rawness of her grief.

When he eventually left her, seemingly replete with the directions and details she had imparted, she felt that the shadow of the dark ages overhung the afternoon, and she mentally chided the child whose imaginings seeped into her waking dreams and forced her back to once upon a time, where giants pelted each other with mountains to create the bottomless, mazarine harbour; home to dauntless sea-rovers and the stirring sagas she had forced herself to recount.

'I must learn to be more sociable', she thought, 'but not to him, and not today'.

With the jetty and the twin quays behind her she strolled past stately buildings and snug clap-board houses, across the River Nid, to the marketplace which was festooned with hanging toboggans, cinnamon flat breads and sweet herbage to mask the smell of sour cheeses and the bundles of dried fish which hung like slithers of leather on the gaily-clad stalls. As the brilliancy of the pale midnight sun began to dip into the charcoal fire that was the night sky the child became more insistent, and so the woman indulged her by stopping to watch a pantomimic display of dancers in national dress.

The men in their cut-down tall hats, curious capes and buttoned trousers fiddled while the women danced, jewel-like in their dark blue serge skirts, embellished, after the old Norwegian patterns with scarlet and green embroidery around the hem. Full sleeved white chemisettes and scarlet bodices laced with silver and ornamented with brooches, enhanced their fairy tale appearance, which was topped with gaudily embroidered kerchiefs atop thick golden braids.

'Come dance', they said, reaching out their gaily-clad arms. 'Get up! Get up! Get up'!

Natural reserve overcame her desire to throw herself into the melee and she shook her head. But their cavorting lifted her sombre mood, and cheered and fortified by the otherworldly spectacle she forgot the tales she had been told of the great metal monsters which spewed legions of spectres on Trondheim. She diverted herself from the horrors he had suffered in this very marketplace, commanded and presided over by Olav Tryggvason; sword in one hand, cross in the other; his bronze eyes fixed on the gaily painted fairy tale houses, doubled and reflected in the waters. She didn't want to think what he had thought; feel what he had felt, when legions of soldiers swarmed, desecrating the sanctuary of the synagogue and cutting down anyone who stood in their way. He had skied over the mountains to Sweden, and thence to the horrors of war. And now he was gone and she wished him back. This was why she was here: to connect. So, she gave the child full reign and allowed her imagination to rest on Bestemor's house, and to the *Huldrefolk* who dwell under the seventh mountain visible in the blue distance.

They had taken a rough cart or as he called it, a *Stolkejaerre* for the last leg of the journey to Bestemor's house. Colder and colder grew the air as they left behind the lush meadows of hawksweed, cranesbill and cloudberries into glacial snowfields and mountain plateaus watched by snowy owls and ravens.

'Listen Aleese, to the lapwing cry 'thief, thief'. He stole the Virgin Mary's silver scissors'.

She listened, and she looked, taking in the gorgeous colourings of the sky and long dancing clouds, beautiful beyond description. She saw the sheen of glittering snow on craggy cliffs and her eyes scanned the horizon for lynx and reindeer and wily Arctic foxes.

Once a bold blue-grey arctic hare blocked their path.

'Look, look at the rabbit. Look at how white he is', she squealed.

'A Rabbit? No Aleese' he gasped, feigning surprise 'she was one of the *Huldrefolk*'? Did you not see her hiding her cow-tail behind her back?'

'*The Huldrefolk?*'

Feigning shock he asked 'do you not know of the Huldrefolk'? Let me tell you a story': And he told her how, once upon a time, God had come to visit Adam and Eve when she was bathing their many children, including those of his first wife, Lilith. There were so many that she bathed her own and left her stepchildren dirty.

'Hide them' said the wife to the husband, 'for God will punish us'. But they could not hide their neglected children from God, who asked 'Are these all of the children'?

'Lilith'? Interrupted the child. 'Who is Lilith'?

'We don't interrupt', He chastised her gently. But as you ask, she was the first wife of the first man. So wicked was she that God changed her into a wild-haired night demon who kills babies in their sleep and feeds on their flesh'.

Seeing she was afraid he distracted her: 'and what do you think happens next, in the story'?

'Eve lies' ventured the child.

'No, she doesn't, Aleese. She tells Him that the dirty ones are hidden'.

'What does Lilith do'? She searched his face; her eyes intent.

'For her children? Nothing! She cared nothing for her children'.

'And what did God do to her children'?

He said:

What man hides from God, God will hide from man, and the dirty children became *De Underjordiske* – the ones living below the ground. And these lost souls remain under the earth, venturing out to cause mischief and to bring humans to come and join them in their misery. The mountain-taken (as they are called, Aleese) are lured by the *Huldrefolk's* wiles. The lucky ones are given magic dishes which turn to slabs of earth and pine cones.

'And the unlucky ones'? The child feared the answer, but she had to ask the question.

'Eaten alive'.

'Are they evil'? She was sure that they must be.

'Some', he said, searching for the words:
Tusse-folk, haugfolk; in English you might call them goblin or trolls. They catch and cook unruly, greedy and lazy children and feed them to their husbands, the *Huldrekarl*, and sometimes they steal away a human child and replace it with one of their own *Huldrebarn. Huldrebarn*, Allees?

'Children'? She ventured, reminding herself never to interrupt again …

'Wicked, ugly children' he smiled. 'Which you are not, *Litten Dukke*. So you have nothing to fear'.

She did fear though, and he knew it, so he changed the subject again:

'And these' he said, pointing to two jagged pinnacles, 'are troll men, *Tusser* who were turned to stone for quarrelling at a wedding, and here are the Seven Sisters, made rock for refusing to dance with the devil…'

In that moment she knew that what she had seen had not been a hare but a Huldra – not mountains, but maidens, petrified by the devil's envious wrath, and as the air grew ever-colder she wished herself in the safety of Bestemor's house.

'Will we be there soon'? As they turn a corner in the forest, the child had seen a vision from a fairy tale.

It stood at the end of a single-track road, serenaded by cascading water and birdsong in an amphitheatre, lined with ferns and forget-me-nots at the centre of a forested mountain beyond the town of Hell. It was made of wood, the outer walls fir trunks, and the gabled roof rough planks, with foot-thick sods of earth, lichen, reindeer moss and birch bark to fill the cracks. The green door opened onto a large room, the walls of which were covered with wooden boards festooned with thick embroidered hangings. No carpets covered the wooden floor, but rough rugs of egg-blue, emerald and scarlet served to brighten the boards and keep out the cold. In the corner a cauldron filled with a savoury mess of fish and potatoes bubbled on the rough-hewn open fireplace, the flames of which were inextinguishable – or so it seemed. Fresh cloudberries and cream sat on a table which was painted red to match a battered dresser adorned with mismatched pottery. The benches upon which she was invited to sit were Scandinavian blue and scrupulously clean. To the child's mind it was an impenetrable fortress: a refuge against the forces of chaos and darkness outside.

She remembered the heat of the room and the warmth of the welcome, but her mind's eye flickered to the grotesque wooden figures, *Huldrefolk*, dozens of them, hunched and unspeakably ugly in parodies of national dress crouching on the cornices around the room. Monstrous families fished in the pots, and warmed their misshapen feet beside the fire. They hung from the single window by their cow-tails, and perched in the rafters, watchful and waiting. The biggest of them rode on carved wolves, using vipers as the reins and digging their hooves into the flanks of their hideous steeds to drive them ever forward. Some had claws and some fangs. All had hideously deformed faces, jutting jaws, hooked noses and impossibly protruding eyebrows. As the sky dimmed to midnight pink and turned to a kaleidoscope of electric blue and green she saw them stir and turn their malevolent eyes upon her. Countless others awakened underground, sharpening their weapons, ready to take her to the world below, home to the diabolic Lilith and her monstrous misshapen brood.

In mute panic the child ran to him. He understood her wordless terror. Safe in the circle of his arms she listened to his comforting tales of once upon a time and long, long ago…

The woman remembered those stories as she pulled her coat closer to shield herself from the arctic, late afternoon air. She chided herself for experiencing the same thrill of fear she'd felt as a child, but she couldn't shake a brooding premonition of doom. 'It is light' she consoled herself. *The hudrefolk* cannot tolerate the light. He had told her so, once upon a time …
    'When the world was very new', he'd said:
… the Jotun, ice giants were fashioned from frozen vapours in the yawning void between the realms of the spring and winter'. Among these was the swarthy Yotun woman, Night who rode a gigantic black horse named *Hrimfaxe* across the skies, daring the sun to shine. And in this darkness, caught between Heaven and Hell, *the huldrefolk*, angry and resentful created chaos wherever they roamed. Odin hunted them as his prey, and sent out his warrior maidens, the Valkyries to light up the skies with their shining armour so that the *huldrefolk* could no longer conceal their wicked ways. And then he sent Denning, the Dawn to court the Jotun woman and in time they gave birth to a son, Day who charged across the heavens; light shining from the radiant mane of his white horse Skinfaxe. This is why we have midnight sun and dancing lights. They keep *the huldrefolk* at bay'.

The woman smiled weakly to herself. She had allowed herself to dwell on the fallen and forgotten children of Lilith and it had unnerved her. She fancied she heard the low subterranean shriek of *the Huldrefolk*, horrid and harsh and echoing below her feet.

'Imagination and exhaustion' she rationalised, dragging her eyes away from the dancers and fixing them on the copper-green spire, and rose window of *Nidaros Domkirke*, the medieval, blue-grey cathedral, dedicated to St Olaf and built over his bones.

'Light and Churches', he'd soothed the child:
They will hurl rocks to the sound of church bells, but they can never go inside', for God has banished them, just as the Norse gods made Nature rejoice when they banished the darkness in Norway. They fear Saint Olaf. He is their greatest adversary, for he tricked *the Huldrefolk* into building the Domkirke. In front of her she saw its soaring arches and countless hideous gargoyles, perched on flying minuets hanging vertiginously on the intricately carved front transept. Behind it the emerald sky blazed like a living flame – a celestial lightshow, illuminating a fiery path for fallen warriors to travel to Valhalla.

She felt herself silently mouthing the words: 'they fear the light'.

'Not all light', said a voice in her ear, close and horrible and all-knowing. She smelled it before she saw it. A rancid aroma of chewing tobacco and earth and something else too horrible for her mind to dwell upon emanated from the unseen figure, filling the sea-fresh, snow-washed air. She forced herself to look at what she sensed was unspeakable danger she saw the American, but not the American as she remembered him. His well-padded frame looked diminished and his malevolent eyes, wily and cruel, blazed with a preternatural spite.   'What did he tell you, Allees'?, he said, in a perverse mockery of the much-loved broken English voice which signified safety and home.

'They own the hunting and the forest', he had warned the child:
Only the foolish would build on the dwellings of the Tusse'. You must tap the cornerstone three times with a stick or they will tear up your house or burn it down... Blue light indicates their presence. You must never, ever follow it. But we are safe in Bestermor's house; see the circle of ash around the hearth? They cannot come within it.

'There is no happy ever after', said the thing sitting in front of the woman. 'He is dead and you are dinner'.
A strange, flickering cerulean light seemed to emanate from its inhuman pores, and dribble out of the bulbous and misshapen nose. Streams of dark azure light shot up into the sky from the clawed fingertips to meet the jade and enflamed brilliance of the northern lights; a vortex of infolding fire throwing the dancers into kaleidoscopic cameo.

Desperate for the company of humans she dragged her eyes away from the drooling *hulderkarl*, but the dance had changed. Demonic chords, minor and monstrous shot like sparks from the violin, the *lur* and the *langeleik* in an impossibly frenzied tempo, worthy of Walpurgis Night. Each man began by seizing his partner's hand, and dragging and twirling her, more and more violently with one arm, and snatching her around the waist to save her from being hurled to an untimely end at the abyss at the end of the world. The women, first bashful then leering spun impossibly, seemingly taking to flight. The fanged and feral men flung them off, continuing to revolve around their screeching partners. Like comets they rushed around the circles, leaping in the air and slapping the soles of their wooden feet with the palms of their petrified hands. All were crude and unkempt. Some had cloven hooves. All had cow tails, which they used to whip up a frenzy and drive her with a ridiculous rushing speed to the centre of their unhallowed circle. As the world spun out of focus she realised that she was being dragged to the World Below.

She felt something strike her back and realised that she was being hung on a hook made of impossibly sharpened reindeer antlers. She heard the hiss of air and bubbling of blood as it pierced her lung. Intricately carved knives, their handles made of reindeer horn flashed as they opened the woman's abdomen and *hulderbarn* grabbed at the viscera, squabbling and ripping at the meat as they forced it into their voracious jaws. She screamed until her tongue was first pulled and then ripped out, and as they methodically and impassively butchered her she gagged on the metallic smell and taste of her own blood.

A female expertly popped her eye with a horned thumbnail and threw it to her foul child who leered and sucked on it contentedly. *Værsågod?*, snarled the indignant mother, shocked at the ill-manners of her whelp. *Tusen takk* growled the grotesque child, disgruntled at being interrupted from savouring the gory delicacy. Satisfied that it had observed at least a semblance of table manners, its mother returned to her task of dismembering the living meat.
'Don't waste any' growled one of the larger of the *Hulderkarl*, beating what was left of her with a club to tenderise the flesh. The whack, whack, whack of his cudgel punctuated the chatter of the charnel house in time to her failing heartbeat. She felt what she assumed to be her kidneys being scooped out.
    'These will make a succulent stew for the elders and we can cure what is left for picnics'.

Her remaining eye was proving a little more difficult than the first to remove. Tutting, the huldre called to her husband for assistance and he managed to extract it using a fish hook to dislodge it from its socket and the blade of his knife to lever it out.

As the dragging, terrible darkness seized her, in the midst of the frenzied mass of blood and bone she had become, the woman's last sentient thought was that she was being eaten alive.

Meanwhile, in a clearing outside of Bestemor's house, where snow, like molten lava magically changed its hue to reflect the dancing skies, countless wooden eyes and a single arctic hare, disfigured by a bovine tail watched the man and the child walking, hand-in-hand into The Northern Lights to where eternal snows mantle the distant mountains.

Figure 16 Huldrekarl

From the Sky

Glen Supple

Bettelheim leaned toward the sink and splashed cold water on his face. . It was a welcome, if temporary, relief from this morning's tales of woe. He wondered what had got into him lately: he was usually so empathetic to his patients' accounts of what their lives had or had not become—through, so they maintained, no fault of their own—yet here he was resenting them. Hadn't they their own two feet to stand on, the innate wherewithal to avoid danger or bypass self-evident horrors? And might he go on to ask himself if this resentment, this flowering disinterest, was in fact the onset of fear of contamination after all these years?

Having picked up the hand towel, he patted his wet mask of newfound cynicism dry and walked back into his office.

His desk was a mess. He contemplated it for a moment before nudging its contents back into some kind of order. Half satisfied, he checked his watch and was pleased to find he had twenty minutes to himself before the next session; ample time for a coffee and a smoke. A red smudge teased his peripheral vision as he reached for his cigarettes. Glancing across the room, he saw hanging from the coat stand his last patient's scarlet cape and hood. He shook his head as if to earn support from some unseen sympathiser then picked up the phone to his receptionist. 'Sweetheart, will you please call Rose and tell her she left without her cloak?'

'Of course. Right away.'

'And a coffee, please?'

He lowered the phone, sat back in his chair and sighed. He looked at the cape again, draped from the hook like a great clot of blood, and contemplated early retirement. Even he couldn't determine why he'd become so jaded, though the accumulation of dark pasts and haunted presents certainly played their part: Rose's forest wolf-men for one; and the waif whose two step-sisters bullied her without rest or remorse; the brother and sister whose memories of being locked up by an old woman with hunger in her eyes and drooling lips still soiled their dreams; the girl who'd been woken from the longest sleep who could not, or perhaps *would* not, adjust to the way the world had changed from how it was before she dozed; and the sad, little man whose seemingly inconsolable source of pain had been his pocket-sized stature, and the name he'd been given by his, clearly, cruel parents. 'I'm not a thumb!' he'd raged through tears one afternoon. 'Is that all I was to them, a fucking *thumb*?'

Bettelheim drew his eyes from the coat stand and spoke into the phone a second time. 'Carol,' he started, halting, unsure he was doing the right thing given his chosen career. 'Cancel this afternoon's appointments, will you? I'm not feeling so good.'

His drive home was enriched as always by the sounds of his local radio station. Between the records and yet another storm warning, listeners phoned in with their views on the topic of the hour. Today they'd been invited to expound on the current spate of what had been labelled by the media as The Eatings.

Bettelheim despaired. What an ugly phrase. Whoever dreamt it up should be ashamed of themselves. But wasn't it just the way of those whose job it was to write the newspapers, to christen the event with something that could trip easily off the tongue, yet sound tame enough to dilute the true savagery of what had befallen the town, and, *ergo*, sell more copies?

'The Eatings,' Bettelheim muttered as he turned into his drive, as if mouthing it might help him dip his toe into the collective hysteria. 'The Eeeeatings.'

Some feet short of the garage his attention was diverted by his wife standing at the front door. She looked pale and, as far as he could tell through the windscreen, was trembling. He switched off the engine and shot out, his eyes fixed on her. 'Whatever's the matter?'

She spoke slowly and quietly. A man, she began, or rather, a boy, had knocked, and when he'd been told that Doctor Bettelheim wasn't at home, bulldozed his way into the house and demanded that he be allowed to wait for his return.

Bettelheim looked over his wife's shoulder. 'Where is he now?'

'In your den.'

He kissed her forehead and assured her it would be all right. 'Go into the living room,' he said. 'He'll be gone before you know it.'

Pop music filtered from the top of the house as he made his way down the hall; his twelve-year-old son had clearly no school this afternoon. Ordinarily Bettelheim would go up to him and insist he do something useful with his free time, homework or extra study, but today there was an intruder to deal with. He discovered him dressed in expensive clothes standing by one of the tall den windows, glaring up at a sky that had begun to honour the promised storm. Bettelheim could tell he'd physically declined since his last session, so much so he might have been someone else.

'How did you find my address?'

His fury was sufficient to startle the boy, who turned sharply, his face as white as the clouds were black. He shook his head while his lips twitched to shape an answer. It came finally, weakly. 'I'm sorry. I... I shouldn't have, I know, but please, Doctor B, there was nowhere else.'

Bettelheim set his professional restraint against a more personal outrage. The latter won out. 'You can't just turn up here out of the blue. This is my home, Jack, not some drop-in centre. And to *push* your way in, frightening my wife?'

The boy lifted his hands as if to repel further reprimand. 'I didn't mean to do that, honestly. I just needed to get in, to see you.'

As tears ballooned in the corners of Jack's eyes, Bettelheim allowed his anger to subside enough to gesture at a chair. 'Sit,' he said, his tone not altogether accommodating. 'Do you want something? Water? Or a cup of tea?'

'No, thank you, I...' Jack glanced backwards and stared again through the window. The clouds had morphed into thick patches of spilt ink, and rolled slowly to announce the first rumblings of thunder. His expression might have been a mirror to them.

'I'll give you five minutes and no more,' Bettelheim said, choosing to remain standing. 'Then you're gone.'

Jack smiled momentarily. It was more out of politeness than anything else, for the look in his eyes betrayed a terror so deep-seated it was a wonder he hadn't been found curled up in a ball. Bettelheim read the signs and softened. 'All right, let's hear it.'

A wall clock's ticking announced the best part of a minute before Jack spoke. His voice sounded no louder than his breathing, but his message was clear. He was afraid he was going to be found; for the long chase to be over; for his pursuer to finally have the last laugh and crush his dreams. He was afraid that today, after all the months avoiding discovery, slipping through the net, he was to be vanquished, leaving his mother to mourn his passing; her little tiger nothing more than a photo on her mantelpiece. Most of all, he added, quaking, one finger pointing upward, he was afraid of the sky.

Bettelheim followed Jack's third glance at the window. It might have been midnight outside if the clock hadn't just turned half past two. The low rumbling had conceded to a first triple-crack of thunder, and shards of rain began to smack against the glass as if begging to be let in from the noise. The doctor listened to it all for a moment, and then, for no good reason even he could think up, his thoughts turned to The Eatings.

The initial reports had reached the papers six months ago, hitting page one from the outset in ghoulish, red-lettered headlines. People were being eaten, snatched through the windows of their houses by some unknown force and devoured. Witnesses described huge half-seen shapes descending from storm clouds, while others swore blind the Devil himself had more to do with it than most gave him credit. The stories of this thing or that thing perpetrating the atrocities grew more outlandish as the numbers of the eaten increased, and the occasional snapshot or video showed only blurred images from which no form could be clearly identified. A few of Bettelheim's patients had their own theories, of course, which only aggravated their neuroses, but none knew better than the boy who'd come to talk about his uncontrollable impulse to steal from others, the boy who'd kept the real truth about The Eatings close to his chest through his own guilt, the boy who was now beside himself with fright in Doctor Bettelheim's house.

'You're afraid your crimes are catching up with you,' offered Bettelheim, his mind returning at last. 'Is that what all this is about?'

Jack looked to the floor and chuckled. The doctor's diagnosis had certainly hit a nerve, yet it sounded so ineffectual in light of the truth he couldn't help but mock it. 'Catching up with me?' he sneered. 'Like the greengrocer collaring some half-starved dope for lifting one of his apples? Catching *up* with me?'

He threw himself against the chair and surrendered to full laughter. His body jerked grotesquely against the cushions as though he were being electrocuted – and enjoying it. Bettelheim watched him coldly, unmoved. He'd observed this behaviour more times than he cared to remember, but today his subject seemed doubly unhinged. The resentment he'd felt over the sink in his office returned. Where there it had been a subtle niggle at the back of his head, a trifle even, here it had become a far more conscious, malignant ache. His mouth curled in disgust as he watched Jack rock from side to side in his growing hysterics. He wished he could snatch one of the cushions from behind the boy and press it to his barking mouth. All these years he'd tried to help these people, dilute their agonies, cure them, and here was one, perhaps no less eager than the others to do likewise if given half the chance, laughing at him in his own house.

Bettelheim felt something far more tangible than fear of contamination infect his bones. It seemed to radiate off Jack as sharp as pins and dig into his marrow. It was a notion that something appalling might actually happen, something that Jack had brought with him; a shadow with revenge on its mind and no thought to who or what might be wiped out in the process.

'So this is your giant, is it?' he asked walking to the window, looking up into the black in an attempt to quell an unreasonably powerful dread.

'I wouldn't look out there if I were you. Not unless you've got a strong stomach.'

'He's tracked you down?'

'You bet he has, but he's not getting me. He can take his storm-disguise and go jump in a lake!'

As Jack's deranged laughter resumed, Bettelheim noticed in the window a reflection of someone standing at the door he'd forgotten to close. 'Phillip, go back upstairs, please,' he demanded, turning.

His son shook his head. 'I don't like the thunder, Dad. It's weird. Do you hear it?'

'It's nothing. Now go back to your room and I'll be with you in a minute.' The child stood mesmerised by the giggling, twitching figure in one of his father's chairs. 'Phillip, I told you to –'

'Okay, okay! I'm going!'

The sky boomed and dashed the rain harder against the glass as Bettelheim rushed across the room to shut the door. It met its frame sharply as the twelve-year-old's trainers drummed up the steps beyond it. With the premonition of encroaching horror having bitten out a further chunk, Bettelheim turned to his patient and informed him that he would have to leave immediately.

'No way was that five minutes, Mister!' protested the other, jumping up, cushions tumbling. 'How is that fair?'

'I'll make time for you at my office tomorrow. Just ring first thing and tell my receptionist I said so.' Without waiting for his answer, he moved toward Jack and reached out to take his arm. As far as he was concerned his role as comforter was over for today and replaced by a far more primal need to protect his family from whatever possessed his intruder. Above him, the roof shook so thoroughly from the violence of the thunder its tiles clapped together like an applauding crowd. The boy cried out, yelped, pulled himself from Bettelheim's grip and ran behind the desk.

'Look, Jack, it was wrong of me to agree to this. It's my mistake, and I apologise for that. But you have to go. My son needs me.'

'My mother needs me too, you know! I'm all she's got! What good am I to her if I'm swallowed up?' He flapped his hand wildly at the window and ducked as low as he could behind the desk.

Blood-red newspaper headlines crashed into Bettelheim's memory, spinning into place like he'd seen in a thousand movies. 'So, The Eatings – they're your fault?'

'No, no, no! I accept no responsibility for his actions! I mean, who can tell a giant what to do? Not me, mate! I can't help it if the greedy bastard devours whoever he finds!'

'But it's you he's been looking for, house by house?'

'Do you know how rich he is? You've never seen so much gold. Why should he care if one or two bits go missing, honestly?'

A roar of something like thunder vibrated through the walls. One of Bettelheim's framed certificates jumped from its hook and shed broken glass across the carpet. Jack crawled into the recess under the desk and whimpered like a scolded dog. His patience at an end, Bettelheim leapt round and dragged him out by his collar.

'Hey, you can't put your hands on me! That's assault! You could be struck off!'

'You're a trespasser,' growled Bettelheim through bared teeth, 'I can do whatever I want.'

Jack kicked and flung out his fists as he felt himself being dragged across the floor. The bulb in the ceiling began to flicker as irregularly as the lightning flashed outside. 'You took an oath,' he sobbed, choking. 'You have to help me.'

Bettelheim reached the door and opened it with one hand. He tossed the sack of skin and bone into the hall where his wife was already standing, disturbed by the shouting and the storm.

'Doctor B,' the boy tried again, 'you have to go out and talk to him. He'll listen to you, you've got the qualifications. Tell him I have a... a thing, a problem; that I can't help stealing. Tell him it's out of my control. I'm a... you know, what you called me once from your book—a klepto-*whatsit*-maniac! Tell him I have to take special pills, or something that makes me do things! Anything!'

The heels of Jack's boots squeaked against the marble tiles as Bettelheim hauled him toward the front door. 'Open it!' he shouted to his wife. 'He's leaving.'

A cacophony of rain, wind and thunder flooded the hall as she did as she was told. After another minute's struggle Bettelheim finally brought Jack to the threshold, and then, using all his strength, swung him round and made a first, merciless attempt to push him out. As Jack grappled to cling onto the door frame, a monstrous sound of snapping wood and shattering glass rushed down the stairs – followed barely a second after by the scream of a child.

Bettelheim loosened his grip on Jack and paid no mind to his scrambling back toward his den to hide. All his attention was on the scene outside the door, on the charcoal clouds that appeared to have at last started to back away from the house. He listened to sounds from inside them that reminded him of colossal teeth grinding against flesh, against bone, against everything he and his wife had lived for during the last twelve years, and wondered what kind of nightmare could make them.

He took a step closer to the doorway and looked out over the debris of the demolished window on his lawn. The last drops of cold rain splashed against his face, some of them red, while his wife began to sob quietly behind him. He remained as fixed as stone in the rectangular frame to study the sky, praying for sunlight to breach the darkness and brighten up the world again. And then, sinking to his knees, his wet, pink-washed face cupped in his hands, his breathing as hard as his lungs could bear, he shook his head slowly from side to side and prepared to take his place amongst Rose and her forest wolf-men, the waif with the two step-sisters, the brother and sister who dreamt of a witch, the girl's agonised awakening from years of slumber, and the sad little crying man whose cruel parents had likened him to a thumb.

Figure 17 Evil Beanstalk

Jack the Giant Butcher

Gary McKay

Jack the Swift swung in his rocking chair and looked at his family. Children, grandchildren and even a few great-grandchildren filled the great hall of the castle. When he was a boy, he could never have imagined owning such a place. It would have been as impossible for him to become a great hero or marry a noblewoman like Jill, yet here he was, surrounded by his loved ones. Jill sat on the chair beside him with Simon, the youngest great-grandchild, on her lap.

Simon yawned and rubbed his eyes.

'I think bedtime is calling for you, mister,' said Jill. She was old, but Jack thought she was still as beautiful as the day he had first met her by the well at the top of that hill.

'But I want to hear the giant story,' said Simon. 'Please, please, please?'

Jack and Jill exchanged a look. Jack shrugged.

'You have to go to bed straight after,' said Jill. 'Okay?'

'Okay!'

'Well,' said Jack. He cleared his throat. He had told this story countless times and he never got sick of it. After all, it was the reason that all of this existed. This was how he'd become the great hero.

The chair cracked.

The giant's eyes had been so big and it had taken so long to die and his mother…

Crack, crack.

What sound had she made as she had died?

As long as the chair did not snap.

Jack shook himself. Where had all of that came from? His mother had died in her sleep and she had made no noise, really.

'Jack,' said Jill. She looked concerned. 'Are you okay?'

'Don't worry, dear,' said Jack. 'I just got lost in my thoughts for a bit. Now, let me see… It all started with some magic beans. I was on my way to market with my cow, Milky-White, when I met an old man, who was probably a wizard and…'

Jack paused.

The hall had suddenly grown silent. It was not a gradual quieting, either. One second there had been a tumult of noise, the next, silence. An impossible idea entered his mind, a terrible, impossible idea that he would not waste his time thinking about. He kept his eyes on Simon. The hall might well have gone quiet to listen to the story.

That was not unlikely, was it? It was an important story. It was the day became a great hero and it would live forever in songs and stories. He opened his mouth and closed it. Wasn't it?

Jill was looking at him oddly now and her smile seemed almost cruel, which was as impossible as the idea growing in his mind. Her smile was always full of life and warmth and was one of the wonders of the world. It was why he had fallen in love with her, so very long ago.

She pointed to the hall.

'No, I don't want to,' said Jack. 'Please don't make me.'

Simon now had the same grin and he, too, pointed at the hall.

Jack slowly turned to look at the hall. It was empty. That was impossible, but it had happened. Maybe a wizard had been here or…

Crack, crack and snap.

Jack spun around. Simon was dead, his neck twisted to an impossible angle and, worst of all, he had died with that awful grin on his face.

'No, please, don't make me go back…'

Jill put a finger to her lips. She reached her hands around her own neck and began to twist it. Her neck went crack, crack and snap, and the grin remained. The sound was deafening in the silence of the empty hall.

Crack, crack and snap.

It cracked and snapped on all sides.

Crack, crack and snap.

The ground began to shake and it felt like the world was about to split apart.

Crack, crack and snap.

Jack's neck was going crack, crack and snap and he screamed and screamed and…

*

Jack woke up in his prison cell. For a moment, he was confused. Then he remembered. He was going to lose his head. It was funny that you could forget a thing like that, even for a moment.

He rubbed his neck.

He had dreamt a lot since that day. Sometimes, he could remember his dreams vividly. Other times, it was like trying to catch raindrops during a storm. Even if he caught the odd thought, it dissolved immediately. Today was the latter and he was glad. He often woke during the night shivering and covered in sweat. Guilt did that to a person.

Guilt sounded an awful lot like crack, crack and snap.

Two of his favourite childhood heroes had been Reginald the Bold and Mervin the Brave. Reginald had knocked out a fearsome giant with one punch and burned her with her frightful children, while Mervin had killed several giants over the course of his life. Those great heroes fought and killed the giants and mounted their heads on their walls. The giants were terrible beasts and their slayers were great heroes and that was all there was to it. They were not consumed by guilt as he was. That did not happen in their stories.

The giants did not take so long to die in the stories, either.

The trial had been brief. There had been an angry crowd and an even angrier prosecutor. Jack had admitted his guilt and contested none of the charges. In fact, he had not said a single word, except for 'guilty'. The public had cried for his head. The prosecutor obliged. All of this because of what had happened on his third descent from the sky; the day he was meant to become a great hero.

Crack, crack and snap.

It should have gone differently. The first two trips had been thrilling and exciting. They had made Jack wealthy and he had heroically outrun a giant; no one had died. But on the third trip…

Marko Blunderbore, the King of the Giants had died. He had been chasing Jack who, this time, was fleeing with a magic harp. This, he would later learn, was one of Marko's most valuable possessions. As he descended, Jack started thinking about what title the people would give him. Jack the Swift had a nice ring to it.

Jack had reached the bottom and yelled for the axe. His mother threw it to him, and with five rapid swings, the beanstalk had fallen, Marko with it. That should have been that. The beanstalk was gone, the giant would die and Jack would marry Jill and live happily ever after. The heroic tale of Jack the Swift and the King of the Giants: a fine story for future generations

Except…

The giant's neck had gone crack, crack and snap when it hit the ground. It was an awful sound that the prosecutor claimed had temporarily deafened everyone within a ten-mile radius. The earth had shook and, for a moment, Jack had thought that it was all about to end. Maybe the earth would not stop shaking until it split apart. A part of him had even thought that that would not be so bad, compared with having to deal with the thoughts festering in his mind; these were not the thoughts that a great hero was supposed to have. But the earth hadn't split apart. The thoughts took root and, fed by guilt and pain, they were quickly all consuming.

Marko had taken so long to die, so very long. Jack had held his hand as he died. The giant's hand was bigger than Jack's face, so he had to grip it with both of his hands. No one should have to die on their own; that's what his mother had always told him. Jack held Marko's hand, listened to the giant's death throes, and stared into those big eyes that had once been so full of life and came undone.

He started to cry. Marko had just wanted his property back. The giants had hidden themselves away in the sky to get away from all of the awful stories about them and Jack had stolen from their King and killed him. Heroes did not do that, but villains did.

'I'm sorry,' said Jack. 'I'm so sorry.'

The giant opened its mouth and closed it. Jack could have sworn that the giant was grinning, somehow, despite everything.

Then the giant died.

Jack kept hold of the giant's hand and looked at his mother. He had done this. He had invaded the giant's house, repeatedly stolen from him, and now the giant was dead. He had always thought of the giants as monsters, but he was wrong. He had never been so wrong in all of his life and if he could have given his own life to bring Marko back to life, he would have done it. But Marko was dead, and that was that.

At some point, Jack had let go of the giant's big hand, a hand that would never hold the hand of another living being. He might have started crying again if the guards had not arrived at that moment. His mother fought them off for a while with her axe and, eventually, they had cut her down. He was not sure what sound her body had made and that bothered him. It was another stupid, pointless death. It should not have been like this.

Crack, crack and snap.

The door to Jack's cell swung open and two guards walked in. The guards frowned. The cell stank and it was initially a struggle to keep the contents of their stomachs down. Jack had lost all track of time in the dark and had long ago gotten used to the terrible smell. Suddenly a guard hauled Jack to his feet and would have immediately fallen over if one of the guards had not grabbed him. Food, water and sleep had been hard to come by however long he had been down here. With the help of the guards, he slowly left his cell.

*

The walk from the dungeons was both the longest and shortest of Jack's life. An eternity and a second simultaneously. It hurt his head if he tried to think about it too much, so he stopped. He had enough to think about, anyway. He was not sure what was going to happen to him after he lost his head. He would die, yes. What else though? Were any of the gods real? He hoped so and, yet, he had doubts.

Maybe there was nothing. Maybe all of the stories and gods had been lies. If the stories about the great heroes were lies, anything could be a lie. The gods and goddesses, the noble wizards, all of it could just be one big lie. Maybe the axe would swing, his head would roll and that would be that. No big revelations, no family reunions, just... nothingness. At least that would end the awful guilt.

He shivered.

Suddenly, he was outside.

The light was so bright and intense that he almost passed out from the shock. He would have screamed if he had the energy. If the guards had not been carrying him, he would have fallen over. The crowd was roaring and chanting and, aside from the giant's awful death rattle, Jack had never heard a sound like it. He wondered if Jill was down there. He hoped not. She did not need to see this.

A moment later, they had become one voice and it chanted: 'Butcher, butcher, Jack the Giant Butcher.' He had never heard his name said with such disgust. Jack the Giant Butcher. Yes, he supposed that was a fitting title.

The guards dragged him with ease, as merely skin and bones now. He was little more than a ghost, really. The crowd roared with laughter and Jack joined in. Why not? If one cannot laugh at his own execution, why bother turning up?

A short while later, his neck was placed on the chopping block. He wondered how many people had knelt like this over the years. Beside him, someone was saying something. Jack was not listening. He tried to open his eyes again and this time he kept them open. The pain was incredible, but these were his final moments and he wanted to die with his eyes open.

There were so many people. He did not think he had ever seen so many people in all of his life. If he had the strength, he would have given them a wave, but he found that he was unable to lift his arms.

His mother had not screamed when she had died. That had been the worst thing. She had just looked sad. Jack thought that people should make as much noise as possible when they went. It let the world know that they were not going to go without a fight.

Crack, crack and snap.

Jack hoped there was something after this, that it was not just nothingness. He wanted to find the giant and apologise. Of course, that would not fix things, but that did not mean apologising was a waste of time.

Jack realised that he was afraid.

The din from the crowd was louder now.

With as much strength as he could muster, Jack said, 'Jack was nimble, Jack was quick, but his brains were no bigger than a thimble.' It was barely more than a whisper, but that did not matter. Nor did it matter than it did not make any sense.

He realised he had no idea what had become of his old friend, Milky-White. He hoped that someone had taken her in. Maybe even Jill. That thought made him smile a little.

As he smiled, his gaze fell on a small old man that stood at the front of the crowd. The old man seemed familiar, for some reason. He was not sure why. Perhaps he had been at the court, but then why did Jack remember him amongst all the others who came to witness his trial?

Cold metal rested on his skin for a second before it was lifted.

The old man smiled and Jack remembered. He was the wizard who had sold him the magic beans and he had the same cruel smile that Jill had worn in his dream.

Jack gasped and was so astonished that he did not even realise that the axe had begun its descent.

TALES FROM THE HOOD

Figure 18 Wolf in Red's Clothing

A Family Dinner

Janet Cooper

When I awoke, it was dusk. The muscles in my legs ached as I swung my legs to side and pulled myself up off the couch. Living in the middle of nowhere has its downsides; it means you have to walk everywhere. Mother had left a note on the kitchen counter instructing me to take Grandma her supper.

'Oh, not again!'

The note was propped against a small, woven basket lined with red cloth. Inside was a container of onion soup.

I pulled on my boots and swung my long crimson cape over my shoulders. The silky satin ribbons felt smooth as I pulled them to my neck, and wrapped them tightly around my fingers and into a bow. The cape fell over my arms, and my finger-tips pressed against the cushioned velvet, tracing the neckline until they found the hood. I tugged it over my head and the furry edging tickled the side my cheek bones. It forced my hair forward over my eyes, and I had to tuck it back into the hood. My long, red gloves slid easily over my palms and up to my elbows.

I grabbed the basket and pulled open the cabin door, peering out into the gloom. The black outline of the trees stood still, frozen. Their frosty, crisp leaves glistened in the moonlight. A shiver slithered down my spine, top to bottom and steam escaped from my mouth and nostrils when I breathed. The pungent smell of lavender overpowered the garden. It was intoxicating and made me feel queasy so I hurried out of the garden.

Twigs cracked and snapped beneath my feet as I hiked through the thicket on my way to the footpath. The further into the woods, the darker it got, but I much preferred the deep woodland smells: the musky leaves, the sage, and the sweet berries. I clutched the handle of the basket tightly, and one of the unravelled wooden strands pierced my glove and finger.

'Ouch!'

The finger part of my glove became damp, so I stopped, slipped off the glove, and sucked my finger. A light breeze made the tree branches sway, gently. They cast waving shadows on the shiny, icy mud. White flecks of snow started to float slowly towards the ground. Beside me the undergrowth shook and I squinted as I scanned it. My heart skipped a beat.

Pull yourself together. You don't want to look too keen.

I slid the glove back on and carried on walking. Leaves crunched behind me and I paused and turned. The sickly-sweet fragrance hit me and lingered in the air. That confirmed it, he was here. I grinned.

'You don't have to be shy, Adney. I know it's you.'

A tall, dark figure rose from behind the bushes, and walked slowly towards me. His long, wavy hair was hanging wildly around his shoulders. His pale skin stood out against the dark grey evening, but his cheeks burned in embarrassment.

'How did you know it was me, Scarlett?' he smiled and flashed his bright white teeth. I skipped towards him and stroked his face. The short bristles on his chin scrubbed my fingers.

'I knew it was you, my love. I could sense your presence.' Our eyes met and I pressed my lips against his.

'Why are you out here, in the woods, Adney?'

'When you told me earlier that you walked this way in the evening to deliver supper for your Grandma, I thought I would check you were safe. There's been some strange things happening, so I'm here to protect you.'

'That's so thoughtful.'

'I couldn't have my girl walking through the woods alone, with these mysterious disappearances. Bain disappeared last night, and Peter the night before.'

'Well, I must do something in return for you.'

We set off walking together. The forest path led down into a valley. A cluster of trees formed a canopy over the footpath and a row of sharp icicles, clung from the entwined branches, waiting to be freed and slice through the air like a guillotine.

'What delights are in your basket?' Adney asked.

'Onion soup today.'

'Onion soup is my favourite!'

'In that case, my love, you must have some. It's still warm.'

'But it's for your Grandma.'

'There's plenty! I'm sure she won't mind.'

We sat on a tree stump still sheltered and Adney helped himself to the soup.

'This is so good!' he exclaimed, exposing the contents of his pallet. A strip of onion escaped and rolled down his bristly chin, and then fell onto his cotton shirt, leaving a greasy stain. Adney didn't seem to notice and continued to slurp down the soup like an animal. Finally, he stopped slurping.

'I'm so sorry, Scarlett,' he gasped. 'I've eaten it all; I couldn't help myself. What about your Grandma?' He tilted the empty container towards me.

'Don't worry, come with me to Grandma's house and we'll explain. I know she'll understand and I'm sure I can rustle something up for her once we're there.'

We walked to Grandma's together. The path started to steepen and soon we were exposed, no longer sheltered by the trees. The snow was falling heavily now. An untouched, thick dusting covered the footpath and our feet padded through, sinking deeper with every step. The cold nipped at my nose, and my feet tingled as my boots gaped at the seam and allowed in the melted snow.

We talked about family; I knew my Grandma would just love him. Adney said that the most important time in his house was family dinner so that they could all sit down together and share.

'I love a man with values.' I told him.

We soon arrived at Grandma's wooden cabin. The snow clouds broke and the moon shone its light through the already gaping door to Grandma's cabin. I pushed it and it creaked.

'Grandma, it's Scarlett,' I said, as I headed inside. A strange moan came from the bedroom.

'Wait here, Adney.' I walked to Grandma's bed to check on her.

'You're weak. You need to eat.' I said stroking her head. 'Oh, and I've brought a friend, Adney.' Candles flickered in the window of Grandma's cabin as the snow-storm picked up its pace.

'She wants to meet you, I gestured him into the bedroom. Grandma, lay in her bed covered by a duvet and multi-covered crocheted blankets.

'Adney, talk to Grandma.' I instructed.

Adney sauntered towards Grandma. 'I'm very pleased to meet you,' he said politely. 'I've heard so much about you.'

'Well come, sit, and tell me about yourself, my dear.' Grandma croaked. All that was visible was a white bonnet. The dim candle light made it impossible to see her properly, only her large, dark eyes peeped above the covers.

'What's that smell?' Adney whispered. 'Does your Grandma have a dog?'

I had moved back towards the bedroom door, and didn't bother answering him.

Adney approached the end of her bed and perched on the end.

'Well, I'm Adney, and I know your Granddaughter. I live in the village. I'm eighteen, and my dad is a blacksmith.'

Adney was staring at Grandma. His began to screw up his face, and he squinted his eyes. He moved his head closer. Grandma sat up and dropped the cover from her face and revealed black fur, sharp teeth, and huge sharp claws. His eyes widened and he jumped from the bed and started walking backwards.

'Scarlett, there's a wolf, get out of here,' he yelled.

He looked over at where I was stood, in the doorway.

'Run!'

I clutched the doorway, tightly. A rush ran through my body and I was doubled over in pain. My knees gave way and I landed on the ground. Shooting pains soared through my arms and fingers. My bones grew and poked through my skin. They cracked loudly and I screamed. Agonising pains pulsated through my legs and I laid flat on the floor, face down, convulsing.

'She's always late, she's new to this!' The wolf croaked, now standing on its hind legs, beside Adney.

'Scarlett!' Adney yelled, running to my aid and crouching beside me. 'Are you okay?!'

I tilted my head towards him, and he stiffened. Blood-shot eyes glared at him. My jaw dislocated itself with one swing, and my chin, jaw and nose stretched forward. Adney fell backwards and scrambled.

'What's happening?' he shrieked. Black hair carpeted my body until I was unrecognisable. White fangs exploded from my mouth and pushed against my chin. Finally I wriggled my already stretched toes and they cracked into place. Like a lightning bolt, I was on my feet and back in front of the doorway.

'Scarlett, is that you?' A terrorised Adney whispered. I snarled and looked towards my Grandma.

'I brought you your favourite for food, Grandma. Meat. Matured for eighteen years and stuffed with onions.'

Adney turned pale. There was no escape for him. Grandma was behind him, I was blocking the door. He dropped to his knees and then slowly sunk to the floor.

Grandma and I circled him, sniffing the air. 'He smells good,' Grandma howled.

I could hear his heartbeat, smell his blood, and feel his fear. My senses heightened and saliva dripped from my mouth.

'Oh, God! Why are you doing this?' he asked. His eyes were wide and watery.

'There's nothing more important than family dinners.' I reminded him. He rolled into the foetal position, crying, and accepting defeat.

'I hope I'm not too late,' a sweet but firm voice said. I jumped around and tilted my head.

'You're just in time, Mother.'

'Oh, good. Nice and fresh,' she said, licking her lips.

'Yes, and it's your turn to get supper next month,' I said.

The Tale of Red Riding Blood

Alison Younger

There once was a girl with a hood that was red,
Who embarked on a trip to see Grandmamma fed,
'Don't stray from the path, or you could end up dead'
Shrilled her mother, a crabbit old dear.
Red gave her a look; she wasn't impressed,
And turned on her heel feeling suitably dressed.
Then she held up her chin, and stuck out her chest
And marched to the forest, devoid of all fear.

In the dark of the woods, she heard a strange sound
So she screwed up her eyes, and peered all around;
'Young lady, come sit beside me on the ground'
Said the vulpine assassin, his jaws in a leer.
She took it all in; her heart starting to race,
And quick as a flash, she smashed in his face
With a wrench that she kept in her Killer's Tool Case
Lodged deep in her basket, should victims appear.

For our Little Red was not what she seemed.
Her wild acts of carnage could not have been dreamed
By her gran or her ma, whose head she had steamed
After cutting her throat with a knife.
In fact, in the basket, the head bobbed about
Midst the tools of her trade, to slice, slash and clout
Those who crossed on her path, when she was let out
Of the cage she was kept in; the murderous fiend.

As she warmed to her task, the wolf howled in pain
With her sharpest of knives she exposed his wolf-brain
And licked on the blade, using blood to sustain
Her energies, frenzied and wild.
Then she opened his belly, and pulled out his liver

Unable to stop a delectable shiver
As his entrails fell out and slid in the river,
Which ran, red with blood by the murderous child.

Then she flogged him, and flayed him, and danced in his blood,
Til' perchance, a good hunter appeared in the wood
And rushed, as he thought, to her aid, meaning good;
To save what he thought was a child.
Too late! When he noticed the glint in her eyes
She'd hobbled him quite, with a club to the thighs,
And smiled at her craft, at the look of surprise
On his fast-dying face, with his own axe defiled.

Her blood-lust unsated, she sauntered to Gran's
The remains of her victims ensconced in two cans;
And kicking the door in she snatched two large pans
To cook up a sumptuous meal.
And in went Ma's head (she deserved the first place),
Then neatly arranged around Momma's face
Were bits of the wolf, and fingers (a brace)
From the Huntsman, so recently dead.
Then, into the bedroom she skipped with great glee
And throttled her Granny; a kindness, thought she,
Before she embarked on extreme butchery
And mopped up the blood with some bread.

Her mother consumed; the carcasses chewed
Her work for the day, quite smugly reviewed
'It served the wolf right' she thought, 'he was lewd'
And, as ever, the dutiful daughter
She cleaned up her knives and her cudgels and flails
And left them to steep in two washing pails
'For the slattern' she thought, 'invariably fails …
There is a decorum for slaughter'.

If this tale has a moral, it might as well be
'Don't stray from the path' or you may well just see
A girl in wolf's clothing, or skin, for you see
There's nothing as plain as it seems.

For a hood that is red could be covered in gore,
And that sweet little house, with the fairy tale door
Could well be a charnel house; under the floor
The spoils of the killer ...
Now, don't have bad dreams!

                Thus endeth the tale of Red Riding Blood.

Figure 19 Red's Ahead

A Tale of Sweet Red

Jennie Watson

Once upon a time, not too long ago, a tale of Sweet Red was told. She had blood-red lips and porcelain skin and a tangle of red curls upon her head. In the deepest of the darkest forest she did dwell, imprisoned by barren trees with branches of knives, waiting to strike anyone who passes. Every morning Red would rise and wander through her solemn fortress, singing sweet melodies to the watching yellow eyes.

Our tale now begins of Sweet Red, when upon a fine morning an unexpected event occurred. For a handsome prince from a far off land took upon a long journey to meet our Sweet Red and this is what was said:

'Oh, Sweet Red, I see you there singing beautiful songs which fill the air. Oh, Sweet Red, come forth; I have a favour to ask of you.'

A smile played upon her lips and forth she went to greet the fellow, whom dared to pass into the deep dark forest.

'It is a surprise to see you here where none dare come to brave the path of this enchanted land, but what is this favour you ask, kind sir? I shall see if I can help.'

'I come here in desperate need for my grandmother is ill, you see. You above all know this forest and the stories it tells. I need you to retrieve something to make her well.'

'Why, sir, of course I would be much obliged to help you in this time of need, just tell me what it is that I have to retrieve and I will make haste and fetch it gladly indeed.'

'I know of a tree which grows only here. It bears a fruit with the power to heal. Many noble men have tried to find this fruit but none have ever returned. Sweet Red, I ask if you would be so kind to help a dear sick old woman, to retrieve one fruit from the magic tree.'

The young man looked up with pleading eyes and golden hair, a handsome sight to behold and Red could not resist the pleading of this fair prince.

'I will set off on this quest right away! But in return of this favour I have one to ask of you. Once I return from this journey with success, you will stay with me, fair prince, for I am a lonely young woman surrounded by a cursed land. You would keep a lonesome girl in pleasurable company. As long as the fruit holds power over your dear grandmother, I shall hold power over you.'

The prince pondered this request some time and looked upon Sweet Red. What a beauty she was, and an honor it would be to be at the command of this fine maiden of the forest. His fortune could be a lot worse than that of Sweet Red's request. The prince had heard many tales of what lurked in the darkness of the forest. A once beautiful green city of nature, reduced to rot and ruin. The tale of the watching yellow eyes that followed all whom entered haunted the prince's dreams, for he had been finding the courage to pursue his request for many years indeed.

'I accept your request, Sweet Red, and I wish you luck on your journey.'

'I shall call your name on the second day at dawn and your grandmother shall be ill no more!'

'Oh, I cannot thank you more. I pledge my loyalty to your command. Now make haste my girl and I wish you well and success!'

'Do not doubt the success of this journey, for I am protector of this land, and all that dwell within these trees. Good day, good sir, for now I shall go. Do not lurk waiting within the walls of these trees for me. Go now, fair prince, go!'

And as quick as quick can be the prince ran off to leave Sweet Red alone.

With the departure of the prince and the day turning to dusk, Sweet Red picked up her wicker basket and hooded cloak and set off on the dirt track that awaited her. A path carved by the many kings and princes of old, drawn to the powers the orchard possessed, now blocked by a wall of branches more fearsome than an army of sword wielding warriors, and a barrier for any whom dared to enter.

Red looked upon the vast wall, and pulled her hooded cloak over her curls. Gripping tightly her basket she began her descent. She walked on, no sign of fear upon her sweet face. She glanced to her left and right as the watchful eyes cast a hazy glow upon the path below. Then something remarkable happened as Red moved into the wall. One by one, the branches retreated from their wall, like a commander recalling his company from battle, giving Sweet Red safe passage through.

'Fear not, my sweet and mighty tree, for I come baring good news. I have found a handsome prince for us, and I shall put him to good use. Your light shall fade no more.'

Red plucked an apple from the tree, a fruit plump and golden and set it inside her basket, and off she went, her quest complete, to call on her dear, fair prince.

'Fair prince! Fair prince! I call on you, for your quest has been complete.'

Far off in the distance as he galloped along the vast open plains upon his white mare, the fair prince heard the calls of Red carried through the gusting wind. And as quick as the prince had left the land, he turned and rode ahead. Sweet Red waited patiently for the prince's return.

'The door is open, fair prince. I have something you seek.'

The prince entered the cottage; his gaze fell upon Sweet Red. Her beauty radiated through him, like the light of the midsummer sun.

Sweet Red moved towards the prince, a smile dancing upon her lips. Not the smile of a once fair lady, the smile that touched the coldest of men's hearts. This was filled with a wickedness that a man should fear. Then something quite extraordinary occurred, an event you will not believe. This fine beauty transformed before his very eyes to reveal the monster within. Her tangle of curls atop her head she pulled and tore 'til she was bare and bled. Her porcelain skin began to shed, layer by layer like a wretched snake and black, coarse fur emerged in place. Her mesmerising emerald eyes, a window to the soul, popped out of the sockets just like that and on the floor they did roll. In their place came small beady eyes, yellow, and dark they were!

The fair prince stood and ran to the door, like a scared little mouse he was! But alas the door was locked. Red laughed and, oh, what a laugh! Not the sweet laughter of before, this laugh was shrill and manic. As she walked to meet the prince, she reached a hand to grab his throat and as she reached, her long pink nails fell one by one from her delicate hands and in their place grew claws.

The prince cried out as she grabbed his throat lifting him with great strength. She carried him to an open door and like a rag doll threw him inside. The prince fell with a great force upon the hard stone floor hitting his head. The last sight he saw was the yellow eyes drawing closer to him and then he was gone.

Red feared the prince to be dead; drawing close to his mouth, she breathed a deep sigh of relief. He was just sleeping; she had time to do the deed. With that she pulled out a small crystal vial and placed it by the wound upon the prince's fair hair, his golden curls matted with dark blood. Drop, drop, drop went the royal blood into the vial until it was full. Red stood tall and held the vial to her eyes and smiled, showing her sharp needle teeth. With haste she ran to the orchard, the golden light of the apples fading more with time. Opening the crystal vial she planted three small drops upon the tree's roots. A shining flash of golden light coursed, like blood running through veins throughout the trunk, mapping its way to every branch, giving life to the tree once more.

*

The prince awoke and surveyed his surroundings. Glinting swords and shields of old knights and princes lay before him, abandoned by their masters on the cold and dark floor. The grim fate of their owners was something the prince did not like to dwell on. The air was heavy with death, like the smoke of the wildest fire; he could not breathe for it! Suffocating from the sorrow the room held, the prince reached for the door and was surprised to find it unlocked. Picking up a sword, the prince set off, ready to redeem the lost warrior for whom it belonged.

The prince began along the path of no return, determination fixed upon his deep blue eyes, the yellow eyes of princes old watching his every move. A gust of wind danced around him, urging him towards his goal.

Succeed you must, noble prince. Release us from this torment; let us die a noble death. Our souls can bear to linger no more.

With the pleas etched in his mind, the prince walked on, more determined than ever to rid this land of the curse that was held upon it. He reached the orchard in quick speed; his eyes drank upon its beauty. Vivid green leaves and golden branches, a sad memory of what once was. He took his axe in both hands and raised it above his head.

'I release this land from torment! Let me see the beauty that was stolen from you! Let me see these trees grow lush and green, let the land be at peace once more! My fellow men, whose eyes do watch, let your souls be free to die a noble death! You have redemption now!'

And with this the prince bellowed a mighty roar as one would do in battle. But just before the axe hit the trunk, he heard an old familiar voice.

'My dear boy, stop!'

The prince turned shocked at what he saw, for his grandmother appeared from the shadows, calling from afar. A shawl wrapped tightly around her head and a stick to aid her, grandmother walked towards the prince.

'Grandmother! I do not understand. How did you come to be here?'

Grandmother was at his side by now, shadows masking her old, lined face. 'My boy, you cannot destroy this tree! Do you want your poor old grandmother to suffer so?'

The prince looked upon the old lady, confusion in his eyes, for something was not quite right, you see.

'Grandmother, come closer still. I want to see your wise face lined with journeys and stories told.'

His grandmother moved closer still. The prince took hold of the shawl covering her old face and pulled it gently away. Grandmother looked down at the roots of the tree.

'Oh, grandmother, let me look into those wide old blue eyes, which hold answers to all the questions I have.'

And with this, his grandmother slowly looked up upon the prince. For her eyes were not blue as the sea, they were yellow, yellow as the burning sun, and burned into his soul. The prince fell back in shock as grandmother moved towards him.

'Do you think I would let a wretched prince be the downfall of me? Release this land if you wish, but you, fair prince, will always be mine! That was the deal and it shall stand.'

'RED!' The prince wailed.

And with that, he reached for his axe. But it was too late. Red's claws pierced the prince's heart. She looked greedily down upon the river of blood like a waterfall cascading from the open wound to the awaiting ground below.

What a feast she had!

Whilst Red was preoccupied with the sight of such royal blood, the prince, with every ounce of strength he had left, reached for his axe with one outstretched hand, he felt its grasp. Red looked up, but it was too late. He struck her neck with a clean hit and off her head rolled. He felt the light inside of him fade; he knew his time had come. He looked around to the orchard tree and the sight pleased his dying eyes. The golden light flowing through the roots began to flow through the land. The trees breathed new life lush and green and vivid flowers did grow, the tormented souls of past princes sighed in relief as they flew to their masters of old. The prince smiled one last smile, contentment in his heart, his goal was complete. He could die a peaceful man and, like the snow in the waking sun, he was gone.

The last of the royal blood spilled upon the grass, carving a river red, flowing towards its destination like a slithering snake to meet its prey. And as the blood swarmed the waiting head, Red began to transform to the pale-skinned beauty of before. Like waking from a peaceful slumber, Red's eyes began to flinch, and slowly the long-lashed eyes began to awake. Her eyes still yellow, the only truth of the monster within. And this is where our tale of Sweet Red ends.

Figure 20 Spanner in the Works

WOLFBANN

STEPHANIE GALLON

In loving memory of Robert Parker (1940-2015)

Heed well this tale of wolves and spells
Of girls, and witches brew;
Into the woods, young Red did walk
To a grove where nothing grew.
She sat there long, she sat there still;
Her thoughts, they made her weep.
Alone she cried, and howled, and sobbed,
And soon succumbed to sleep.
And to the dirt, her tears did fall
As she dreamed of happier things.
A flower stretched, it bloomed and grew
As white as angel wings.
When Red awoke, she spied the bud
And picked it from its patch.
She smelled it bloom, and smiled small
And head for home at last.
But a wolf had stopped her in her path
And Red let out a scream.
The wolf advanced, kind eyes glowing bright
And licked her, like in her dream.
The pair played for hours, then days, then years
Until both were fully grown.
They stayed together, Beaut and Beast,
A wolf of her very own.
He kept her safe, and loved, and warm
With a fierceness that could burn.
No man dared near her, but she cared not;
She loved him in return.

SUPERNATURAL

Figure 21 Evil Tree

Figure 22 Doppelgänger Fairy

THE TREE

JAMES CHRISTIAN STRACHAN

Once upon a time there was a town that was always shrouded in night, and the rays of the moon shone out in a soft beam of light that lit the darkness as to a candle in a sunless tomb.

One day, the folk of the town began to notice a great tree that they had never seen before outside the village, whose branches were leafless and whose boughs were as tendrils twisting up to the sky above. The tree was black and terrifying to many, and was curled fearsomely like a half-closed fist. Soon, two riders from the town who were dear friends rode to investigate the mighty structure, yet, when they dismounted their steeds, their hearts were filled with malice and hatred for the other, more than any man has ever hated his brother. Their eyes filled with tears, and they withdrew their swords and killed the other.

Three sisters of the village come to play upon its outskirts stumbled upon the tree shortly thereafter. Intoxicated by its ethereal radiance, they danced in a circle about its trunk, and its refulgent aroma inebriated their spirits. Onwards they danced 'til their feet bled and they wept amain, unable to stop dancing. Never did they move from hence; after a week of dancing, they withered in form and starved 'til death took them.

Two lovers in search for a quiet enclosure in which to frolic came to lie down a while beneath the shelter of its branches, meaning not long for to stay. No sooner had they lain in such a spot did the tree take them. Wrath overcame the two, and with much weeping they clawed at the other until the blood flew, and until little was left of their skinless bodies.

Even the birds that came to perch upon its branches fell victim to its might; their gay song would become a weak and sickly chirping, barely audible, as if they had given up hope to sing. They eventually would stop singing, and would drop to the earth, lifeless.

Soon enough, the townsfolk knew the tree's power. The *podestà* of the town called for the tree to be burned down, and a great mob of men and women bearing fire and pitchforks set about to march to the tree. When they arrived to the tree, they all dropped their armaments in awe of the tree's power, and they were amazed. They then began to disrobe until they were all unclothed, and they set about to make love to the other. Soon there was a great pool of eloping flesh – men and women alike – fornicating violently with no mercy. After some time, the folk began to weep violently, every orifice bleeding profusely – men began to bleed through their eyes with a cosmic dissemblance flowing through them; women's heads twisted 'til they faced backwards; they contorted in agony, and each, in tremendous fear of the tree, fell dead upon the earth. The *podestà*, the leader of the band, decanted his entrails through his mouth about the dusty plain.

Now in that time there was a great fear about the town of this tree, for their *podestà* was dead and there was no order in their society. There were riots, unrest, and civic chaos, for each that had set about to destroy the tree did not return. The townsfolk would argue in the marketplace as to how to rid their home of the tree. Then a young man came to the rout, and he was fair of form and beautiful. He bade them know that he was fresh of mind, and unfoolish, much unlike his kin; he swore by his blood that he would rid the town of the tree. With blessings from the women he rode a white steed to the tree. Dismounting, he approached it.

He asked the tree its name. It did not answer. He asked it how it came about to this foreign land; what was its measure, its meaning, and its impulse. The tree was silent. Finally, he asked the tree to show him its power. A foul wind blew through its branches, and the boy fell to his knees with silent weeping. He was granted many visions in his mind of rapine, destruction, death and bloody apocalypse. When he awoke, the earth was still and natal. The boy made love to the tree and died thereat, and the tree begat him a son.

The son of the tree and the boy was a twisted abomination; an unspeakable abortion of flesh and twig, skin and bark, that was an amalgamation of all that is abhorrent and menacing in Nature; no larger than a bairn and with slanted and distorted form, it screamed and writhed in newbirthed agony, and with unprecedented speed the creature limped into town.

All was asleep in the town; husbands laid next to their wives, brothers to their sisters, lovers with lovers. The daughters of the village slept in silent ecstasy.

The creature, son of the tree, snuck silently into each house and raped the virgin girls that lay within sleeping. The creeping tree, stained with hymenal ichor, ran back to its father outside the village – its duty done, it shrivelled and died, and became one with the roots of its sylvan progenitor.

By morning, each father would wake to find his daughter bloodied and impregnated by an unnamed horror. Out of the cleft of woman's thighs writhed tendrils of bark and xylem, twisting and undulating violently, and with much screaming and bloody torment the girls would beget a son; unhuman, arboreal and smoked with bestial hybridity. Oftentimes during birth the size of the spawn would tear the flesh of their clefts up to the navel, killing the mother in unimaginable agony. When born, the spawn would leap at the closest thing, usually the daughter's father, and tear his flesh asunder 'til his life left him.

The gathering spawn would flock from village to village about the land beyond the mountains, raping and impregnating the women and killing the men. Blood was entwined with tree once more. Fathers would throttle their daughters before the tree children could violate them – those that were neglected such mercy often died from birthing the twisting sylvan horror. Word travelled to each hamlet of the coming horde; with sharpened swords and edged falchions the villagers prepared to do battle with the swarm. They met bark with bladed metal and branch with fire, but seldom did a village fend of the invaders. The daughters were raped once more, and fathers' throats were bloodily torn from their necks.

Those with wit prayed and sacrificed to Apollo in the temple, the God of Elysium so well renowned for his vengeance upon acts of rapine throughout the land. He was called *Vindicator of the Virgin* by many, and was loved by all. One day, when hope seemed its faintest, a thunderbolt crashed upon the altar of the temple, and out of the fire came Apollo. The townsfolk clothed him in regals, fed him wine and victuals, gave him his short sword and sent him off to rid the land of the tree spawn that raped their daughters and sisters, for Apollo was known as a revenger of the raped.

The folk of the land bade Apollo do battle with the tree children with the sword and the spear and the silver trident; to lay waste to those that robbed their sisters of their girlhood. Apollo refused them, and sought a better way to dissolve the land of the spawn.

When Apollo reached the tree that had caused such mischief, the tree did not intoxicate him. Apollo was immune to its lure, and he did not die.

Apollo withdrew his short sword, and, through thunder and lightning, storm and tempest, he cleaved from the mighty tree a goodly portion of wood, from which he carved a flute. The flute was bathed in Elysian majesty, and its sound was so gentle it could tame any beast and soothe the bitterest of hearts. He blew the magic flute, and the tree shrivelled and died.

Thus liberating the village of the tree, Apollo set about to soothe each tree child to rest – he sprung from village to village, hamlet to hamlet ridding the populace of the xylemic invaders that came to violate all purity. He sounded the flute mightily and he sounded the flute softly, and soon, all the trees withered into the ground, and were as dead. Therefrom, the virgins of the village lived in peace beyond the pale mournful mountains, and Apollo watched over them as guardian and protector.

So thus Apollo sung the trees to sleep, and bade them lie down in the marshèd earth, from which no violation of innocence ever sprouted again for as long as Apollo reigned in Elysium. The stars were hung in the endless sky like dotted fireflies gliding above the night ocean. He took the magic flute, so gentle in ethereal brilliance, and hung it up in heaven in the Temple of Morningland.

Figure 23 Tooth Demon

Hannah Smith

Nay, but hear me,
On this peculiar thing.
Why do sad women wander?
And happy men sing?

A girl was I
When he found me here.
He would hold me close
And whisper 'My dear!'

Seafarer was he, and
From the sea I came.
If only I'd known
He was seeking but fame.

And so through the wood
I was frantically wooed,
Soon caught in his arms
Was I ardently subdued

As we did dance
By blazing fire,
Skin on skin
Scorched by desire.

My love was he
And the first
But naivety
Was to be my curse.

For a ship it came

Mulier Maris

Late in the night.
From my bed he crept
By candle light...

The moonlight
Watch it fall
Upon my love
For him I call!

In the woods
I do wander,
My call echoes
O'er hills yonder.

But where is he
Who stole my heart?
Long gone now
For he did depart

Faster than lightning
O'er the raging sea.
How I hear the Sirens,
Their call to me.

'Our dear sister
Come to us,
Leave the land
Lest thy heart should rust!'

So atop that cliff
From there I dived,
To save a girlish heart
That shall never be revived.

THE GHOST WHO DIED

ALEX MILNE

There was once a boy called Abe who was born in a strange land many miles from here. Where he lived, the sun came up at night and the moon shone through the day, and trees kept their leaves in winter and shed their bark instead. Abe was not tall, nor was he short. He was neither handsome nor particularly ugly, and neither stupid nor clever. He was simply an ordinary boy. But where he was born, nothing was more to be despised than being ordinary.

The people of his land competed with each other to display the most unusual attributes, or to acquire the most remarkable talents and to distinguish themselves from their countrymen to the greatest degree possible. Abe's mother, Jean, had eyes at the ends of her fingers, allowing her to look backwards or around corners, while his father, Philip, had groomed his hair into a stiff, cross-wise Mohican so strong he could use it to fasten screws. Their garden grew trees seven hundred feet high that had just a single leaf at their tips, and Abe's family ate from a table so high that everyone had to jump in order to reach their plates. This usually resulted in a terrible mess on the floor, but like most families, the scraps were eaten by their pet Kigatoos, a creature which hopped about on two legs, had no arms or wings, but had a neck like elephant's trunk with a mouth full of sharp teeth at the end.

Abe was his mother's eldest child and when he was a baby, Jean loved him with all her heart. 'I wonder what wonderful talent he will have,' she wondered as she cradled him in her arms. 'Will he grow to thirty feet tall or learn to predict the weather from the beat of a butterfly's wings?'

As Abe grew however, he displayed none of these talents. It became clear that he was as plain and as ordinary as it is possible to be. His parents had three other children: a daughter with four arms who could play the guitar and the saxophone at the same time; another who toyed with differential equations instead of dolls; and a son who was born without limbs, but could affix legs of metal that allowed him to run faster than any other boy.

Embarrassed by her son's lack of distinction, Abe's mother would beat him and demand that he devote himself to learning an exceptional talent.

'Why can't you be more like your brothers and sisters?' she would ask. 'They are all as different as can be, yet you are the only one in this whole land who is ordinary!'

Abe would shrug and tell her he could only be what he was, at which point his mother would throw her hands in the air and despair of her eldest son.

Whenever visitors came to her house, Jean would hide her ordinary son in a cupboard and pretend she only had three children, whom she would proudly show off. 'Don't you have four children? Her visitors would ask. Each time she would answer: 'No. I have but three.'

While locked in the cupboard, Abe would listen to the rapid metallic rattle of his brother running, while freeform acid jazz bubbled from one direction and the scratching of chalk on a blackboard came from another, as his sister solved another hyperbolic triple integral. He would hear his mother tell her friends she had no fourth child and feel ashamed of himself, he who embarrassed his mother so much that she denied his existence. Yet what could he be but himself? For Abe's talent, unknown to his countrymen, was no less extraordinary than those of his siblings, for only he among all the people of the land was capable of accepting himself simply for what he was.

One day, Jean hid Abe away and forgot to bring him out again. Her sister was getting married to a frog and going away to live at the bottom of a pond, and the wedding required very special preparations that took up all her time, while her husband was far away, building a boat made of solid gold for the King, who was revered as the maddest man in the kingdom. Her three talented children helped her out, running errands, preparing music for the reception and applying stochastic algorithms to work out the seating of guests both human and amphibian. Jean had never been happier or more proud of her three children. Her fourth child, Abe, gradually faded from her thoughts.

As for Abe, well, he was quite used to being locked in cupboards and over time he had built secret doors that led outside, so he could get out and play in the sun when everyone thought him hidden. Yet when he saw how happy Jean was without him around, he decided the time had come to run away forever. Who could love a boy so plain, he asked himself? His family would be happier without him.

He travelled across the country seeking work, but at every town he was shunned for being so ordinary. This did not worry Abe, for he was quite used to being treated in this way, yet every rejection caused a drop of bitterness to seep into his soul. How could his countrymen be so callous?

A farmer with fingers that grew in place of hair employed Abe to spread slurry on the fields with his hands, and docked the rent of a pig sty from his pay, and an undertaker who could win any game of chess in a single move made him live in the mortuary while Abe washed the bodies of those who had died of the plague. Although Abe worked as hard and as well as he could, his employers would be rid of him as soon as they had an excuse, for they felt embarrassed at having someone so ordinary working for them.

While Abe was away, Jean's husband Philip returned from building his golden ship and asked where their other child was. Jean hesitated, as though confused between a dream and a memory, then shook her head and said: 'No dear, we have but three children.'

'But what of our second son?' asked Philip. 'The boy who was ordinary?'

Jean gasped and put a hand to her mouth. 'Do not say such things! To think we could have a child that lacks any special talent. You should be ashamed of yourself.'

Philip hung his head and apologised and wondered at how he could have imagined such a thing. Had he really been away for so long and had the work been so hard? Nonetheless, he couldn't help but notice how his wife seemed somehow distracted. She would spend hours staring at cupboards and restacking shelves as though she had lost something, but whenever he asked, she would give him a vacuous stare and deny anything was amiss.

By chance, Abe found himself in the same port city where his father had built the boat of gold. From hearing the tales of sailors from distant lands, he learned of a place called Swindonia: the most boring place on earth. Perhaps there, he thought, I will finally fit in.

He spent a year cleaning out the city sewers, saving his pennies until he could afford to buy passage on a ship to this fabled land, where everyone was ordinary, just like him, and not strange and cruel like his compatriots. Perhaps there he could find someone to accept him for who he was. Maybe there he would be loved.

The skipper accepted his money and gave Abe a berth on his ship, but insisted he stay in the bilge and refused to allow him out. One night, a storm struck the ship, driving it into the jagged teeth of a reef which ripped the timbers from the hull. As the boat filled with water and sank, the crew escaped on lifeboats, but Abe was trapped in the bilge. He clawed and screamed and begged for someone to help him. No-one cared to hear his pleas and help.

And so it was that Abe was dragged down to the depths of the ocean where he drowned.

As his lungs filled with water, Abe's soul became filled with bitterness and anger, which weighed down his soul like lead. His spirit tried to float away, but Abe's fury bound it to the earth, and so the boy became a ghost and made his way out of the waves and back to his homeland, for ghosts are drawn to wherever the bitterness that binds them to the world originated.

*

The afterlife of a ghost is a painful one, for everything in the mortal world is unnatural to them and causes them pain. The air suffocated Abe like the seawater in which he'd so recently drowned, the rays of the sun burned and the breath of the wind was like the scrape of sandpaper on his pellucid face. His soul felt only the desire for revenge, to punish those whose cruelty had seen him trapped in the form of a ghost.

Abe found the crew who had abandoned him when their ship foundered, and followed them on their next voyage. When the ship was many leagues from the nearest coast, he caused the winds to die away for three months until ship was becalmed. All ships carry a community of rats, and as both men and vermin ran out food, Abe spoke to the rats and organised them into an army.

'There is plenty of food on board,' he told them. 'It is simply stuck to the bodies of the human crew.'

At Abe's encouragement, the rats swarmed over the crew, biting and gnawing and tearing the flesh from the bones of the sailors while still alive, no matter how they struggled and screamed. When the sailors had been eaten, Abe allowed the winds to return and the boat sailed back into port, where nothing could be found but a crew of fat rats.

At the port, Abe found the Royal Warden of the Waterways who had made him drink sewer water while cleaning the pipes. Each year, the Royal Warden made a ceremonial inspection of the plumbing beneath the city, but this year, as he descended, Abe distracted the man guarding the manhole and caused a gust of wind to blow it shut so hard it became stuck.

Abe went to work on the pipes he knew only too well, clogging them so that vast quantities of sewage were directed to the place where the Royal Warden was trapped. The level of excrement gradually rose and, no matter how the warden struggled, he could not escape and was drowned.

Abe continued to travel the country, exacting retribution for all the wrongs suffered during his life. The undertaker who made him live in the mortuary woke up one morning to find his baby daughter eaten by his own kigatoos, and the farmer who made him spread slurry on the fields fell into a bag of fertiliser, which rolled into the river and burned away his flesh until his entire body dissolved. Yet no matter how grisly or gruesome the fate of his victims, he only felt his hatred of life and of mankind intensify, and this bound him more and more closely to the mortal realm.

Inevitably, Abe was drawn to his home in the forest of seven hundred foot high trees, and the mother who had forgotten her own child. He hovered around the house, flitting from room to room in the dead of night and sliding through the cracks in closed doors to watch while his family slept.

The house was a place of grief, for while Abe was away, his father Philip had been executed by the King after the golden boat he built sank on its first voyage. The reading of Philip's will was met with much puzzlement, for his last request was that his property be divided equally between his four children.

'Four children?' Jean had asked. 'We had but three.' Yet as she spoke, she felt a whisper of something within her mind, a rumour of a forgotten love and a memory of a dream that was no dream.

Abe watched his family mourn as he drifted through the house and plotted his revenge. He pondered how he could turn his siblings against each other, so they could use their talents to destroy themselves, yet he saw how much they loved each other and knew such a plan would fail. Instead, he considered causing a fire to burn down the house with his family inside, yet when tried to kindle a flame, he remembered the comforting feel of his mother's embrace and the music of her laugh, and the burning anger in his soul dimmed.

While her son plotted his vengeance, Jean found herself dreaming strange dreams. As she slept, she would be visited by a fourth child, a son she had once loved but had allowed to pass from her mind. She would see him sweep from room to room, his once-plain face disfigured by years of rejection. Her heart broke for this lost soul who was once her son, and she tried to take his diaphanous form into her arms, as she had once done when he was a boy, but of course Abe simply passed through her body.

Then, one morning, Jean woke with a plan. Memory and dream at last became untangled and she knew the ghost who haunted her sleep was the son she had forgotten to love, and that only she could release his spirit from the bonds of bitterness that bound him to the earth. She organised her three other children and put her plan into action.

Using her talent for mathematics, Abe's sister composed a song of intricate harmonies and rhythms so complex their construction required seven-dimensional Euclidean algorithms. Her sister applied her skills with guitar and saxophone to learn the piece and her brother learned to use his fast metal feet to play the drums.

Unlike the living, there is only one type of music so loud and violent that even ghosts are moved by it, and it was in this style that Abe's family wrote the song in his honour. Today, it is known as Death Metal because of its impact on those who have passed away.

Late one night, Abe's family set up their instruments and started to play the song. At first, the ghost tried to ignore the music, but as the harmonies swelled and grew, and as the rhythms yielded rhythms of their own, he found himself dancing along, his spirit called away from the bitter memories of his life and entwined with the music, which was unlike anything anyone had ever heard before. And over the polyrhythmic sweep of that sound, Jean keened and wailed her grief for the death of the son she had once forgotten.

With each phrase Abe's burden of hatred became less, with each crescendo his attachment to the material faded. He realised the song was based around three chords that spelled out his name: A, B and E. The tune had been written for him, the complexity and skill of its construction was in his honour.

As he heard his mother's grief and the emotion with which his siblings played their instruments, Abe saw his family's flaws for what they were: the blindness and stupidity that every human shares, that he knew he too possessed in equal measure. In his time as a ghost, he had come to see how short and desperate the lives of mortals are, and now he came to realise that he could accept them for what they were, just as he had always accepted himself for what he was.

And so, as the music grew to its climax, Abe did a very difficult and powerful thing. He forgave all the people who had shunned and mistreated him during his life, for he had learned that it was not enough only to accept himself for what he was, but he must also accept others for the way they are. There is nothing that has a greater effect on the soul than forgiving those who have wronged you, and as Abe gradually relinquished his hatred of the living world, his spirit became lighter and lighter.

And as the last notes of the song faded into the night, Abe's soul became completely unburdened and at last flew free of the earth to journey to the resting place of all souls. And so it was that, at last, Abe died happily ever after.

LOVE AND DEATH

EMMA COLLINGWOOD

We begin our tale in a desolate land where the winters seemed to last for millennia, plunging the world into darkness like a never-ending plague. The sun's visits were scarce and brief and when he did appear to greet the residents of this land, his rays rarely warmed the skin. They were no match for the icy wind that clutched the trees like the cold hands of Death, removing all signs of life from the forest, when the days were at their shortest.

Folk seldom ventured into the forest alone. It was home to many an unearthly creature, which had long since waged an unholy war against humanity, using the dark arts to manipulate these god-fearing mortals. They used them like pawns in their games, and would laugh at the discord they caused. The young ones were the easiest to trick; so fresh-faced and filled with innocence; so wide-eyed and enchanted with thoughts of magic, and of beautiful, impossible things. The fairies felt no shame in luring them away from their kin with promises of wishes to be granted and endless adventures, but the children were foolish, and in need of protection. The wilderness was home to the most evil, most blood-thirsty of creatures, in constant search of mortal flesh to devour.

Some might have said that the people of these parts had no childhood, for the children had no choice but to work the land alongside their elders in order to earn their keep. In spite of this they were happy. They knew no other way of life, were content in one another's company, and loved each other deeply. It was all they needed.

There were two young ones who, like so many of their friends and neighbours, had their childhoods shortened by necessity. They were good people. They had kind and honest hearts, and their friendship was strong. Their souls were woven together like the roots of the ancient oaks buried deep under the earth's surface. Slowly their friendship grew and love blossomed.

It had always been a favourable match: the matchmakers saw it in the stars and indicated their love was a rare, precious gift. But they warned, however, that they must tread carefully, for a union that was not ordained by the gods would end in tragedy. The lovers promised they would obey this stark warning.

The gods were kind to them, for they were strong of faith. The gods blessed them with good health and wealth; loyal friends and long lives. They were thankful, truly thankful, for all the blessings the gods had bestowed upon them. There was, however, one facet of their lives which seemed to be cursed. As they buried yet another child, their hearts began to harden as the familiar scene replayed itself. The tears, the prayers, and the seas of white lilies, plucked from life, as the innocent infants had been. The pain was endless as they lamented time after time. Numbness filled the man and he forgot how to feel. Upon seeing his latest angel as still as though she were sleeping, sadness and anger stunned him, and he could barely breathe. He cried to the gods, begging them to let her live. He pleaded with the gods for mercy: hadn't they always tried to please them?

Tears transformed themselves into anger, as he demanded to know why they had been cursed. What could they have possibly done to warrant such a punishment, and why must they be treated as nothing more than play-things by those from the great beyond? They must be laughing at us miniscule dolls dancing across the earth. They were spiteful; picking their favourites, lavishing blessings upon them, but turning their backs once they were bored. The man had exhausted himself and fell to the floor. It was hopeless: there was nothing more that could be done. Suddenly, a figure appeared before him.

'You are here to take her from us!' He cried. 'You will not spare her and why should you? You would not spare our other children. You have not a heart, Death.'

'You say that you know me,' Death replied. 'You say that I am heartless and care not for the beings I deliver to the afterlife. The truth is I have no choice. I am merely a messenger with no power. It is the will of the gods.'

The hopeless man wept.

'You are an honest and loving man, and the gods pity you,' said Death. 'They have seen how much you have lost, how much you have sacrificed. Despite their power, it is too late. She is gone and they cannot bring her back. They cannot reverse time. They are sorry they could not save her sooner.'

'You are lying, I know it! You *can* bring her back!'

Death shook his head, 'I cannot. My condolences, sir.'

'Please! Please, take someone else. There are evil creatures in this world, Spirit; take one of them instead.'

'I cannot.' Death declared.

Death had been numbed by time, and had learned not to feel when carrying out his duties. Yet for this man, he felt the deepest empathy, for he too had been punished and was destined to walk the earth forever. He had no one to love, and was blamed by all mortals for their losses. He hated the gods for inflicting this punishment on him. Like the mortals, he existed to serve at the pleasure of the gods. For the first time in hundreds—maybe thousands—of years, Death made a choice.

The child would live.

They named her Agnessa, 'the holy one', in honour of the holy force that had allowed her to live. She could not have been more loved or cherished; she could not have been more perfectly made had she been the daughter of the gods themselves. Every day they reminded themselves how lucky they were to have one so beautiful. Never once did they fear that the gods would punish them for interfering in matters beyond the mortal realm. Surely it would be Death who would forfeit for disobeying orders.

The months turned to years, and as they did so, Agnessa grew into a most remarkable woman; all who laid eyes upon her were captivated by her fair countenance and warm, all-knowing, tawny eyes. But it was not only her appearance that made her so exceptional. She seemed to see the good in everyone, even the most petulant and unforgiving soul. There was something other-worldly about her: she seemed to have cast a spell over everyone she met. Some said it was it was a great shame she had been born a woman, for there was little she could accomplish in this unforgiving place. How harsh it seemed, that her fine, delicate hands would be put to work here, as her skin would grow weather-beaten and wrinkled.

The village folk pitied her, for she had no place here but they admired her still - worshipped her almost – some believing she had been sent by the heavens to keep watch over them. Others suggested that as an infant, she must have been captured by the fairies and enchanted—and surely she would lure them all into the demons' clutches. Such whispers of hexes and curses were often dismissed as blasphemy. Surely a girl of such beauty and goodness could not have been corrupted. The ones who spread such lies were shunned into silence.

More years passed and the family's happiness grew still. Now fully grown, it was time for her to leave the nest and find her own happiness. But as the icy sun set beyond the trees, a figure crept slowly into view. Fear filled her father, paralysing his heart. It had been so long since they met, but there was no mistaking him.

'The gods are angry.' Death said. 'They hate us for what we have done.'

'No!' her father cried in anguish, 'you cannot take her!'

'It is not I who can decide. The gods have decreed that you shall be punished.'

'Why now?' The father demanded, his voice falling to a whisper, barely audible above the howling winds.

The gods were furious at the father and Death for meddling in their affairs. They took mercy on the mother, however, and decided to grant her eighteen years of happiness. At the end of the eighteen years, however, the father must be punished for his disobedience. It was the only way.

That night Death took her as she slept. When her mother woke the next morning, he heart broke at the sight; Death took her too. The father wished for death; wished to be reunited with his family. But the gods were vengeful. He would suffer for eternity and not ascend to the heavens. His soul would roam the Earth for the rest of time, long after his body was buried. He would never escape. He would never be forgiven.

The Baroness and the Servant Girl

E.L. Little-Gainford

Long ago, in a land that has since lost its name to time and to bloodshed, there was a Baron who controlled his lands with an iron fist. His people would have rebelled against him, were not for his kind and beautiful wife. Whilst her husband could be cruel, the Baroness was generous and forgiving, and could easily sway her husband's opinion. He was so enamoured by her beauty and youth that he found it hard to refuse his wife's requests.

*

The years passed, as they are wont to do, and the Baroness's looks began to fade. Her golden hair began to show streaks of grey, slight wrinkles appeared around her eyes, and her once lithe figure began to grow plumper. The townsfolk began to notice the Baron travelled alone more often. The times when the Baroness did accompany her husband, they barely spoke to one another. Despite her silence for the man who had once prized her above any other jewel, she still had a smile for her people. The Baroness would wave as they passed children playing on a village green and enquire about the health of her favourite baker and his family. The Baroness, who was still not yet in her fourth decade of life, was ever the people's champion and could still persuade the Baron to be more lenient, using her wit rather than her beauty.

Then a harsh winter came to the land and all began to suffer. Food was scarce and more people resorted to theft in order to feed their hungry families. The Baron, warm and well-fed in his castle, had no pity and began to hand out cruel punishments for those suspected of theft.

On a particularly cold day, the Baron made his usual visit to his most trusted burgomaster and had begrudgingly permitted the Baroness to join him. Whilst the two men discussed matters over hearty ale at the burgomaster's grand house, the Baroness was allowed to wander the streets of the town. She soon came to the town square, covered in thick snow and practically deserted as everyone was home desperately trying to stay warm. Everyone, save the five poor souls still held in stocks in the middle of the square.

The Baroness was horrified. Three men, a woman, and even a child had been accused of stealing and placed in the stocks overnight during one of the coldest winters she had known. The Baroness approached the still body of the child, whose long, matted hair and ragged clothes made it hard to tell if they were someone's son or daughter. She reached out her hand and felt the little one's icy skin. Gasping, she drew back her hand in horror. Then, steadying her nerves, she placed a trembling finger under the child's chin and lifted their head. Two milky eyes stared past her from under half closed eyelids. The cracked lips had turned an unsettling shade of blue. The woman and the oldest of the three men had also been unable to survive the night. The two younger men, though unconscious and losing fingers to the cold, were still breathing.

Suddenly an imposing dark carriage, pulled by horses the colour of midnight, thundered into the square and stopped beside the Baroness. The velvet curtain was pulled to one side and a bejewelled finger beckoned her in. The Baroness's fear of her husband was outweighed by her outrage and sense of justice. She fell to her knees in front of the carriage, begging her husband for mercy for the two men. Her impassioned pleas fell on deaf ears and two of the Baron's coachmen hauled her into the carriage in a manner undignified for any woman, let alone one of noble blood.

A whip cracked and the carriage rumbled off through the town and into the dense forest that surrounded the castle. The Baroness was never seen in public again. Rumours about her fate swirled through the land. Some swore that she had died, some claimed to have seen her in the castle suffering at the hands of her wicked husband. Young Gisila grew up hearing these tales from the women gossiping at the village well, or from some traveller come to trade with her father.

On the eve of her fifteenth birthday, Gisila sat helping her mother prepare dinner. It was meagre fare since her father's business had started to suffer after the Baron's wicked rise in taxes. She sat stirring the pot and daydreaming. The stiff wooden door opened and Gisila's father came into the house, dusting off a smattering of snow that had covered his worn coat. He coughed loudly, breaking Gisila's reverie, and she watched as he eased himself into a chair by the fire. He took off his boots and set them at his side before leaning forward and placing his head in his hands with a sigh.

'Gisila,' he said softly. 'I'm sure you're aware of how hard times have become. I'm getting less business, and less business means less money. Money which we need not just to feed and clothe your brothers and sisters but to pay our taxes. I have spoken to Aldegar, who collects our village's taxes on behalf of the Baron, and he has kindly agreed to a deal that will benefit us both. Gisila will go to work at the Baron's castle and pay off our debt. Not only will I not face the wrath of the Baron, but we will have one less mouth to feed. She goes the day after tomorrow.'

Only a fortnight later a horrible sickness started to spread throughout the Baron's lands, and rich and poor alike took to their beds. Not even the inhabitants of the castle were spared from the fever and within days the number of servants still able to work had dwindled. Gisila had yet to fall ill and found herself taking on many extra duties.

On one particularly stressful day whilst desperately trying to relight the kitchens fire, she noticed the cook arguing with one of the more senior maids. The cook, a robust red-faced man, suddenly pointed to Gisila and roared: 'Well, take her then! She's useless to me when I have to go around correcting her every mistake!' And with that, he charged to the other side of the kitchen and began banging pots and pans whilst shouting at the kitchen boys.

The senior maid tilted her capped head at Gisila and indicated for the girl to follow her. They left the kitchen and hurried through the corridors and up a spiralling staircase to the maids' sleeping quarters. The maid poured a jug of water into a basin and ordered Gisila to wash her hands and face. A fabric bundle was then thrust into her hands. As she changed her clothes from her rough, dirty kitchen smock and into the cleaner maid's tunic and apron, the maid explained that most of the servants were either sick or dead. Women who had waited on the Baroness had been replaced by the younger maids and now there was no one left to do the more menial tasks. There was no one left except Gisila.

Gisila's first chore was to empty the Baroness's chamber pot. She was shown to the suite of rooms belonging to the famous Baroness and left to do her work. The first room she entered was the most public and was where the Baroness would have received visitors, had the Baron permitted her to have any. Treading lightly, Gisila made her way to a door on the other side of the room which was filled with ornate couches and large mahogany sideboards. The next room was slightly smaller but just as dark and grand. This was the Baroness's private sitting room, where the walls were lined with books, their leather spines fading over the years. Between the archaic tomes were two more doors, one leading to a dressing room and then onto a privy, and the other into the bedchamber. Gisila stared at the doors, trying to remember which one she had been told to go through. Was it the left or the right? Taking a deep breath she reached out and turned the door handle.

This room was darker still and it took a few moments for Gisila's eyes to adjust to the gloom. Peering around, she discovered she was not in the Baroness's bedchamber but in the dressing room. Gisila's eyes flitted from mannequin to mannequin, each one draped in gowns of rich velvet and silk. They stood motionless and eerie in the dim light. Suddenly a figure turned and stared at Gisila. Shadows from the fireplace danced across the figure's delicate features; it was pale and emotionless. Gisila gasped and began to back out of the room, muttering humble apologies and stumbling as she attempted to curtsey.

The door shut with a solid thud and Gisila dashed through the door to the bedchamber, her heart racing. She had seen the Baroness, who was most certainly not dead. Perhaps her eyes had played tricks on her, perhaps it was the poor light, but Gisila was sure the Baroness seemed younger than she'd expected.

The Baroness was the same age as the Baron when they'd married some fifty years ago. Gisila's grandmother had been a small child but remembered the pomp and ceremony that had accompanied the pretty young bride when she came through the villages and towns on her way to the castle. Obviously a privileged life of good food, a warm bed, and days dedicated to leisure rather than labour meant the rich lived longer and aged less quickly. *But why*, thought Gisila, *does she seem younger than even my own mother?*

The next day, much to her surprise, Gisila was summoned to the Baroness's rooms once more. Gisila had completed her chores for the morning and was wondering why she could be needed. Was the Baroness going to punish her for yesterday's mistake? When she arrived she found the maid who had collected her in a panic. More servants had fallen ill in the night and there was no one left to dress the Baroness. Once again, there was no one left but Gisila.

'I will fetch her a clean gown whilst you brush and plait her hair,' the maid panted from under a pile of dirty laundry. 'Now, girl!'

Gisila went into the dressing room, whose windows were still covered in heavy drapes and lit only by the fire and a few candles. She mumbled a good morning to the Baroness and picked up a nearby brush. The Baroness's did not respond as she gazed into her mirror and ran her hands over her smooth, tight skin. It was as if she barely knew Gisila was even in the room. The soft bristles of the brush pulled through the Baroness's mahogany curls with ease and Gisila soon set it aside and began braiding her mistress's dark hair. As she twisted the strands, Gisila's brow began to furrow. Before their first encounter she had been expecting the lady to have the silver hair of a grandmother. Now of course she understood that the Baroness had managed to maintain her youthful looks far better than any commoner but there was still something about the hair that made Gisila uneasy.

Gisila was soon given the task of assisting the Baroness more frequently and she began to gain the mysterious lady's trust. One evening, as Gisila brushed through the Baroness's hair before bed, a crafty thought entered the young girl's mind. She began to brush more vigorously. Then, noticing the Baroness was too busy looking into her mirror, Gisila gave a tug on the ends of the hair. Sure enough the Baroness's entire head of hair began to slip away from her scalp. The Baroness's shrieked and her hands flew up to her head; she was not quick enough and it fell to the floor in a tangled heap. Gisila gasped and stepped backwards. She had suspected the Baroness had been using a wig but had assumed it was to hide her greying hair. Underneath, the Baroness was completely bald, but the wig hid an even more shocking secret. Tiny metal hooks were buried in the Baroness's skin around her face. They had been pulled tight, lifting the Baroness's face into a state of perpetual youth, and anchored into her skull. Every now and then, one of the hooks slipped, ripping into her flesh, and now her head was covered in infected wounds and dry patches of blood.

The Baroness was clearly upset and angry, and she fumbled as she tried to arrange her hair back on her head. It was no use and she sighed, defeated.

'What is the point? You have already seen my shame and who is there for you to tell anyway?' The Baroness tried to frown and the skin pulled on the hooks, causing a trickle of blood to run down her face. Gisila gently wiped the blood away,

'Is this how you've managed to stay young all these years?'

The Baroness looked at Gisila. 'You think I am Herleva, the first Baroness.' Gisila looked confused but let the Baroness continue. 'Herleva was the Baron's first wife, the one with the golden hair. It was she whom the people loved, but she died many years ago. The Baron had noticed her getting older and he found he was attracted to one of her maids. He wanted a way out of their marriage and his burgomaster advised the Baron to kill her. At first he could not do it but, on the day she tried to save the peasants in the square, he decided that it must be done. The next day, the Baron dragged his wife down into the castle dungeon and strangled her. Then he buried her in an unmarked grave down there and married her maid. The servants wondered where the first Baroness went but those who spoke out went missing as well.'

'You were the maid!' Said Gisila, shocked at the revelation.

'No,' the Baroness shook her head sadly. 'I am the fifth wife. The Baron soon got bored with his new wife, Sigilind. She had enjoyed her new life too much and had eaten to excess. Her plumpness disgusted the Baron so she began to starve herself in an attempt to please him. It was no use as he'd already found a replacement. Sigilind went the way of her mistress. Ishild was his third wife and the only one to bear him any children, a son. She worried about her figure after the birth of their son. She knew what had happened to Sigilind so Ishild began wearing tight corsets that broke her ribs. When she realised that a young peasant from a nearby farm had caught his eye, Ishild mutilated herself, cutting at her skin, trying to remain slim and beautiful. Three months after her son was born, Ishild died in the dungeons and the Baron married Leutgard, the peasant girl. She was my predecessor and my mistress. I brushed her hair as you have done mine these past weeks. She had tanned skin from working in her father's fields and the Baron thought it made her look poor and undignified. He wanted her to have the pale skin of an aristocrat. It did not fade despite her treatments. She poisoned herself trying to lighten her skin and the Baron led his sick wife down to her doom before coming to ask for my hand in marriage.'

Gisila was appalled. 'Is this why you have done this to yourself? To stay young for him?'

'To save myself. He will kill me as soon as he chooses a younger girl to marry. I should not have married him but I was a servant and could not say no to such a powerful man!'

The two women stayed silent for a moment. After a while, Gisila spoke.

'It seems inevitable that he will murder you.' The Baroness nodded but Gisila raised her hand. 'Unless you kill him first.'

It was now the Baroness who was shocked but after some thought, she agreed to Gisila's plan. The Baroness lured the elderly Baron into the dungeon, where Gisila was waiting with a sword taken from the guard's room. The Baron happily followed his wife, unaware of the danger and thinking that now might be a good time to get rid of his wife with a face like stone.

The Baroness and her husband shuffled into the darkness of the dungeon, edging closer to where Gisila was hidden. Before they could reach her something strange began to happen. Eerie voices began to cry out in chorus and a horrible mist filled the dungeon. The cries grew louder, calling out the Baron's name and for vengeance. Four ghostly figures appeared before him, each with the marks of his hands on her throat. One of the Baronesses pointed at him menacingly and he screamed in fear. Suddenly he clutched his hand to his heart, his face growing red and a look of terror filling his eyes. The evil Baron sank to his knees, his ageing heart failing him, and he dropped down dead. The four women he had so wronged lurched forward and wrenched his soul from his body before pulling him, kicking and screaming, to the underworld. The dungeon was silent again and all Gisila could hear was the thudding of her heart.

And so Baroness Walburga, fifth wife of the Baron was spared an early death. Gisila married the Baroness's stepson, who was now Baron after his father's death. Walburga lived to see Gisila restore peace and prosperity to the land, and she died an old woman, happy in her bed.

THE GLASS COFFIN

DANIEL FARRELL

Long ago, there was a small, secluded village. It was built predominately around a large pond and surrounded by a vast forest. The locals were wary about what lay outside the confines of the society they had created and so very few ventured out. This meant that the villagers were forced to remain in the drab surroundings where the fog was dominant, only occasionally becoming a faint mist.

When Gabriel awoke one morning, he knew at once the judgement that would come to him for what he intended to do that day. There had been word whispered around a select few of a lucrative job on offer in one of the towns on the other side of the forest. However, this would require a three day trip, so he made sure to be up at the crack of dawn.

'Must you go?' his wife asked him. 'I have a bad feeling about this trip.'

Gabriel scoffed at her worries. 'Come now,' he said, 'you know I have to do this. It could be the opportunity of a lifetime.'

This did not seem to comfort her. She grabbed his coat and handed it to him, saying, 'I suppose you're right, but please promise me that you'll be careful.'

'Of course I will,' he laughed.

As they both made their way towards the door, Gabriel picked up an old oil-lantern and lit it.

Immediately upon his exit from the house, it was clear that word about his endeavour had gotten out, just as he had expected. He walked across the village and through the fog he could make out the rare person watching him before retreating back into their home. He knew that they were only concerned about him, but he wished they would be a bit more subtle. Even the few ducks that inhabited the pond seemed to shun his gaze.

Eventually, he arrived at the edge of the forest and stared through the gnarled trees at the shadowy venture that awaited him. Gabriel took a deep breath and walked into it, his head high the lantern held right out in front of him. He made sure to stick to the path; that was the most important rule.

After an hour, the fog showed no signs of lifting and the branches ahead looked as foreboding as ever. Even with his lantern, there was barely any light, making the trek a lot more dangerous than he had anticipated. Just as he contemplated returning to his village, a faint white light caught his eye.

A short distance away stood one of the most beautiful women Gabriel had ever seen. She had long white hair, was wearing a white dress and bathed in the white light. It took him a few seconds to notice the transparent wings behind her. She was a fairy.

The fairy smiled and began to drift away into the forest.

'No, wait!' Gabriel cried out.

Without thinking, he ran after her, disregarding the path. She had gone quite a distance from him now, though, and he tripped as he attempted to keep up. Regaining his posture, he realised that not only had she gone, but so had the path.

The sound of footsteps caught his attention and he turned to look. However, it was not the beautiful lady that was approaching him, but two wolves. One had black fur and looked quite disapproving, whilst the other, donned with grey fur, appeared fairly indifferent.

'Foolish traveller, you venture into these woods without the faintest idea of the dangers,' the black one taunted. 'You're lost, aren't you?'

'No, I'm not,' Gabriel lied, unwilling to let the creature get to him. 'I just stepped away from the path to see the woman and tripped.'

'What woman?' the black wolf asked.

'She was a fairy, I think,' he replied.

'There are no roaming fair folk in this forest,' the black wolf snarled. 'They are confined to an eternal slumber whilst their queen remains encased.'

Gabriel had heard rumours of such beings but had never heard the full story and, despite him wanting to get to the towns as quickly as possible, he was intrigued. 'What do you mean encased?'

'There is a castle in this forest that harbours her forever in a coffin,' he explained. 'She has been there for centuries, but nobody has ever dared to free her. There are whispers that her gratitude would reward the freer for a lifetime.'

'Where is the castle?'

The wolves did not answer, but instead turned and Gabriel squinted, seeing for the first time the faint outline of one in the distance.

'If I free her, do you think that her gratitude would extend to helping me get a job? That's the reason I'm passing through here today.'

The eyes of the black wolf narrowed. 'No good can come from this forest, human.'

'Now, now,' the grey wolf said, 'that's not entirely true. Should you wish to attempt freeing the fair folk's queen then by all means go to the castle; just know that nothing is guaranteed. The choice is yours.'

The two wolves exchanged glances then continued on their way. Gabriel watched them disappear into the fog and stood trying to come to a decision.

In the end, he figured that as he had already abandoned the path, he may as well go further. If the fairy wasn't there, then he'd surely manage to find his way to the towns eventually. And if she was there, then rescuing her from encasement could really help him.

And so, without any further hesitation, Gabriel made his way towards the castle.

He thought of his wife and what she would say if she knew what he was doing. This was the kind of thing that would terrify her – she couldn't bear to even look at the forest. To him though, this was an even bigger opportunity than that of a job. Perhaps the fairy could use her powers to shower him in riches so he could return to the village a wealthy man. The endless possibilities ran through his mind and spurred him on further.

The castle gradually came into focus. It looked like it had been abandoned for many years: the bricks were worn, the windows cracked, and it appeared to be crumbling on one side. The sight of it sent a shudder down Gabriel's spine, but he brushed it off. He had seen a fairy in the woods for a reason and he figured that this was it.

Opening the large oak front doors, he made his way into the bare entrance hall, in which the only decoration seemed to be cobwebs.

'Hello?' he called out, but had no reply.

Gabriel had the urge to run away and never looked back, but swallowed his fear and proceeded to walk down a long hallway where a faint light could be seen emitting from the distance. Surely that must be wear the fairy was.

At the end of the corridor, Gabriel walked into the light which was coming from a large room with a high ceiling. In the middle was a glass coffin where the woman he had seen in the forest was lying, motionless. Her hands were crossed over her chest and she resembled a statue.

Gabriel cautiously tapped on the glass, but nothing happened. Looking around, he spotted an axe perched against the wall. He picked it up and was surprised by how heavy it was. It should definitely do the job. With one swift movement, the blade of the axe hit the coffin and it shattered.

The eyes of the fairy snapped open. Her mouth widened as though she was screaming, yet not a sound pierced Gabriel's ears. He watched in horror as her body crumbled away, as though made of sand. He backed away, yet couldn't tear his eyes away from what he was seeing. A gust of wind caused a nearby window to burst open and Gabriel dropped to the floor to protect himself against the ferocious storm that was now sweeping into the room.

Suddenly, a blood-curdling scream rang out and darkness enveloped everything.

'Gabriel? Gabriel!'

He opened his eyes and steadily got to his feet. He was stood in his bedroom back home. It was the crack of dawn. As he got to his feet, the door opened and someone entered.

'Must you go?' his wife asked him. 'I have a bad feeling about this trip.'

Gabriel turned to her, shaking. His face was extremely pale and sweat was dripping profusely from his brow.

'Why, whatever is the matter?' she asked.

He did not reply straight away and instead pulled her into a tight hug. The mist from outside was clinging to the glass on the windows.

'You know, I think you're right,' he said, kissing her on the cheek. 'I have a bad feeling about the trip, too. I think I'll stay home.'

THE ELFIN-SONG

JOSHUA WRAY

I could not sleep. I had retired to my chamber early but found myself roaming before long, and flickering aimlessly through books in my library. Elizabeth, my child sister, and only true friend, had become the latest victim of an illness in our village. When I was first informed, she was young and strong, whilst carrying a child, and with only half of those falling to the mysterious illness ending in fatality, I fancied she would come through the other side unscathed. However, her health deteriorated at an astounding rate, and the optimism I began with died by my second visit.

That morning had been my fourth. As soon as I walked into the room she smiled widely as I embraced her bed-ridden self. Though I did not let her see as I held her, I was filled with horror at the sight of her, for I had never seen a living person so wretchedly pale. I collected myself, and gave her a look of little fear or doubt. We spent much of that morning holding one another's hand and recalling fond memories of our youth. It was a pleasure to both remember, and to see some of the colour sink back into her cheeks as the sun rose to its height. When she felt she had the strength, I carried her to sit by the fireplace, and we had some soup and bread; the cure to end all illness.

I left her mid-afternoon when she needed more rest. I sensed I had eased her mind somewhat, yet I could not help mine feeling uneasy, for though her spirits were high, her body was to be failing her; I felt the worst was soon at hand.

During the long carriage ride home I felt anxious, and for the rest of the day it did not dissipate. I went about my daily business with a cloud over my head, almost bereaving for someone who had not yet died. After my failed attempt at sleep, looking through the library in search of settling my mind, I turned to my bible and read a few scattered passages—Abraham, the most righteous man. He had every reason to refuse God, to be afraid and turn his back, but he remained ever faithful; the challenge that this life offers, is for us to do the same.

I had begun to nod into a silent dream at my desk when I heard a loud knocking at my door. My faraway self slowly came back to consciousness, and I ran down the stairs, opening the door with grave anticipation. It was a young lad, servant to my sister's husband, who stood in the doorway with a desperate fear, panting beyond control.

'Master Evans, I was sent as once, we fear Mrs Reid will not last through the night'

'Have you sent for the doctor?'

'Mrs Reid begged me to fetch you first, Sir'

'Fly then. The doctor, now!' He rushed away back onto the bench of his master's carriage; and whipping the horses to sudden speed, he raced down the lane to the house of the village doctor. I swung the door shut and ran for my gloves, boots, and coat, then ran out into the night.

Following the roads of the village, noting also the delay that darkness brings to dirt tracks, my carriage would have taken around two hours to reach her home. Knowing that was how long it would take for the doctor to finally tend to her, I could not risk her dying before I had chance to say a final goodbye.

Our village is an odd shape, it curves along a woodland in the fashion of a horse-shoe, yet keeps a healthy distance from the domain of the trees. Elizabeth's home lies on the outskirts of the eastern side whereas I live in our family home to the west. And though no established road of our village leads through the woodlands, all I had to do was run in as direct a route eastwards as the land would permit, and I would arrive in a clearing within sight of her home. I fancied a brisk run through the woods would take less than half the time any other route would take, and so without thought, that is where my scurrying feet led me.

There were legends in the town of an unnamed malevolence within the woodland, and I was told several puerile folk-tales in my youth by my grand-parents; yet I stopped believing in them before I reached the age of ten and assumed that generations ago some child had wandered into the woods alone and fallen into a hidden mire, never to be found again. Of course, there is more romance in fairy-stories than cold, unfortunate events, thus I believed as the birthing of the tales of my childhood. Still however, as my feet bustled through the dry grass and I came to the edge of the woodland, a wild terror came over me. The trees rose up high in crooked shapes and leant down with sharp claws that encroached on me in the stammering winds. I felt as if the ancient horrors of my childhood dreams, of which I could not remember any particulars to, were suddenly renewed with all their horrid pertinence. I almost choked with rising apprehension. But I had no time for such inhibitions, and with barely a pause to gather my composure, I stepped beyond the threshold and into the domain of a deep darkness. Yet something about it felt uncanny, it was as if the trapped autumn air I inhaled, contained the blooms of dry, crispy plants I had never experienced before. I knew not what it meant, I only continued on, running at speeds I had not seen since my younger days; when I and my Elizabeth would race each other in childish play. She usually won, but only by my will for her joy.

As I moved further into the woodland, I soon discovered that the land was not as flat as it appeared from the village, for there were strange, large mounds in the ground all about the thick trees. Some of them bulged to near my own height with tough roots protruding out of them, and to maintain my speed, I was forced to move round in wide and uncertain arks, all the while trying to return myself back to the straight line I in poor knowledge had designed.

My early steps in the face of such unexpected difficulty left me hopeful that I would see her in good time. However, whilst pacing myself and leaving little time for thought I found myself moving increasingly south as the roots and mounds became more perilous to my pace. Whilst still running, I tried to judge within the trees to my left where I should have been according to my line, and as my attention had moved away from my immediate senses, my ears began to hear a distant voice. It startled me to hear such a thing out there, but as I came to a halt, I realised it was not one voice, but many. They were hollow, high-pitched, and in some sort of strange rhythm as they began to surround me. I stepped a few yards forward, listening to the lyrics of the foreboding tone:

With shot aclean comes our mark
We dance and play in the dark
Awake for us light and star
Near we dwell yet sound afar

As I tried to decipher the words, the moon shifted behind the growing black clouds, and in an instant, the woodland seemed to grow in a putrid, exuding darkness.

I stood to hear the high voices for only a moment longer, then paced with all my speed further east, trying to think of nothing but my destination. Faster and faster, around curving mounds and thick jagged roots I moved. I fancied I was going mad, the awful voices came around me from all sides with subtle menace, yet every time it felt unbearably close, and the hairs on my arms and neck burnt with an electric fear, I found a new stride in my step and somehow managed to outrun the growing song.

I ran at my full speed for another mile without hearing the voices until I stumbled over a large, unseen root. But having been moving with such pace I fell through the air and tumbled down a small ditch below one of the mounds. I lost my bearing for several moments as my head spun in all directions and my foot pulsed a cruel throb. And within only a few moments of not moving, those little witch voices came back to me through the vast obscurity.

Motion fade whilst time doth burn
Our sole plan thy will not learn
Our folk in woods grow but small
Yet songs take all for enthral

The voices around me were soft but full of conviction, rising louder with each word.

'Leave me to my grief!' I yelled into the scenery of grim, dead trees. 'I must see Elizabeth ere her passing.' The horrid voices were both north and south of me, yet I found it impossible to tell if they were becoming louder or nearer.

Nevertheless, my destination lay east, and feeling for that brief moment it was a clear path, I rushed up to my feet and ran until those voices became nothing but little choral harmonies in the distance behind me.

I ran with so much desperation that once I felt I was at a distance that they would not once more try to close; I collapsed down to the ground to regain my failing breath. My hands fell onto my knees and all was silent save my panting into the world around me.

A few minutes passed by and I began to feel control of my pacing heart again. Then in some grim declaration, or a march into some impending fate, the voices began to rise again.

'What do you want?' I screamed out westwards towards the sound, 'do not torment the nigh mourning with phantom songs!'

The song continued to rise in both volume and seeming numbers, and I rose to my feet with a panic. Stepping slowly backwards whilst keeping my eyes westwards towards the sound, my intuition told me that though my terror would increase, I was not in imminent danger. For long moments whilst peering towards the sound I saw nothing save the impenetrable darkness, and when I blinked my eyes I saw no difference of light. I looked westwards, southwards, and to the north, and as my terror began to overwhelm me I looked longingly eastward. The dark seemed thinner there, and I guessed I was nearing the edge of the wilderness. I stepped on a few yards and felt a devastating relief come over me as I perceived faintly the candle-light of Elizabeth's home, radiating from the window a warm and homely peace.

But my eyes involuntarily fell backwards as the little voices altogether stopped in unison. And in their place, was a multitude of the most beautiful, and magnificent bright lights I have ever seen. There were no words for it, it was as if my experience of the sun had suddenly become a lie of cold and dim proportion. These lights were small, like stars floating up in the trees; a revelation at last of Empyrium. But as I gazed upon those pure white lights, they seemed to move. It began almost as a swelling of light, like a trick upon my sight in the dark; but they did move, they gently flowed to and fro in the black haze.

I was in awe, it was sublimity at its most terrific. Without a thought I found my feet stepping towards them, and my hand by its own desire reached upwards into the lower branches of a tree to caress one such light. Given that my mind was swimming in wonder, I cannot be entirely sure, but I thought my hand went through the light as I tried to grasp it. I tried again, and again, and soon all the lights around me danced in solitary motions to a strange rhythm. I smiled, almost laughed aloud in the night.

All of the lights became thicker, and denser, and whilst those closest to me began to slowly withdraw, my focus subsequently shifted from particular lights to the image of them as a whole. I threw my hand behind them, attempting to stop them from leaving me, but it caused no such thing. I tried it with another, that too proved useless, and every effort only hastened their retreat from me.

It took much will, in fear of losing them to a new speed, but I managed to refrain from my attempts on them, and in turn their pace remained a steady sway. It became clear to me they were made of something beyond this world entirely as they moved in and out of the trees in magic motion, from five-foot low, right up into the heights of the highest trees. I stepped on with them, all the while awe-struck and swaying my hands like a conductor to the soundless song they danced to. I do not know how long it was that I followed those lights, time seemed both to stand still and yet pass through many seasons. My feet passed over many roots and stumps pursuing of the purest specks of Heaven, until ultimately, I stepped across a brook.

The moment my trailing foot touched the ground on the other side, the lights sharply dimmed, then disappeared altogether. My heart pounded and I could have cried for the emotion that welled up in me quite suddenly. I ran ten paces in search of them, but nothing could I see. I even flung my hands upwards in the hope of disturbing the air to whatever conditions were hitherto needed for their radiance. But it was fruitless; and I fell to my knees in despair.

In the abysmal wood, then, slowly from my dazed reverie, I somewhat returned to myself. I remembered my intention, I remembered my love for her, and my desperation to reach her before she became nothing more than a memory. I glanced hopefully back across the brook, but saw nothing of the dim candle-lights of her windows. And through my unknown journey, I was no longer certain which way was east. A noise fell from my mouth which I cannot describe, and I clutched my shirt by my heart, wishing in my desolation only for the chance to see her one last time.

'Her last breath draws near' a nasally, odd voice spoke from out of the dark. I winced and almost cried. And as anguish took dominion of me, an abrupt starlight shone down through the thorny limbs of the trees, and revealed to me, was the silhouetted figure of a human-like creature no more than two-foot tall.

'How can you know such a thing? I wish only to say my last farewell,' I called out with broken voice and looked desperately to the shadowy figure as it stepped out of sight. A chorus of their song began to sound again in the oppressive gloom. 'Quit your ominous song,' I pleaded to where the figure had stood. 'Guide me back to my sister!'

With shot aclean comes our mark
We dance and play in the dark
Awake for us light and star
Near we dwell yet sound afar

'The souls of the woman and her child are ours, and we take the spoils of our play,' the grim voice returned atop the continuing song.

'Do not play, do not dance, for she is a kind and warm soul; I would do anything to save her from your sport' I cried to all the voices around me.

> *Thou in this dim realm of plight*
> *Save thou not will all thy might*
> *When thy steps fall past the brook*
> *By elfin-shot thy be struck*

'Anything?' uttered the queer little voice as its figure came back into obscured view, and the singing of the crowd consequently came to a halt. 'Greater still, than the high-spirit of a new-born, is the soul of a martyr, for their selfless choice is beyond any measure of purity. If you wish to save her, then give us your entirety, give us the rejection and sacrifice of your being; give us your soul.' The little figure stepped forward with a clenched fist excitedly, and I could hear all around me the other voices murmuring with muted anticipation. I felt so defeated, I coward into a shaking heap in the grass and felt a sharp prick in my ribs.

'Can you guarantee me, they will both, mother and child, live long and happy lives?'

With a solemn tone, it replied, 'that, we *can* promise.'

> *Older we and older still*
> *Souls by us shall do our will*
> *Greater than two of new-birth*
> *Martyrs are of highest worth*

The moon and stars rained a soft whiteness into the woodland, reflecting back to me the whiteness of the being's teeth and eyes as it looked to its companions still singing their strange song.

I thought of her one last time, of her bright and gay smile. I thought of the life-affirming joy in her eyes as she told me she was with child; then of the laugher and waltzing that followed with her husband until the stars rose and swooned. I myself had no such future in place.

And so with a deep, uncontrollable shiver, and one last look at the moon through the malignant trees, I spoke.

'For the safety and happiness of my kin, I will give you my soul; and all that you will…'

Figure 24 The Sorceror

CAST DOWN YOUR EYES

JAMIE SPEARS

Some believed she was born evil.

They said the skies went black at the moment of her birth, and that is why the tribe's holy men named her Ch'agii – Blackbird.

Others believed that she turned to the *án̓t'į̓zhį̓*, to the witchery way, because she could not bear children.

Regardless of how she came to it, all members of the tribe knew Ch'agii was *yee naadlooshi* – a skinwalker. Mothers warned their children that if they saw Ch'agii they must cast down their eyes; for if they made eye contact with the *yee naadlooshi*, she would transform into a coyote, kill them, and steal their skin.

The only way to be rid of *yee naadlooshi* was to say their full name. But none in the tribe dared to – so feared was Ch'agii.

Ch'agii made her home by the river. She would sit and watch from her dwelling as the tribe's children passed to and fro, collecting water.

'Cast down your eyes,' they would whisper nervously to each other. 'Cast down your eyes like mother said.'

Ch'agii would watch them. Watch them and wait.

*

Haseya and her brother were charged with collecting water for their family. Every morning they ventured to the river, their mother's fearful words echoing in their ears: 'when you pass by the home of Ch'agii, cast down your eyes.' So dutifully, every day, they cast down their eyes, and did not look upon Ch'agii.

But Haseya was curious. Curious and brave. Her name means She Rises, and throughout her young life, Haseya had always found a way to rise again, to remain resilient in the face of danger.

One morning, she decided she would not cast down her eyes. Ch'agii was only an old woman, she reasoned; surely there would be no danger in looking upon her. As she and her brother, balancing their water pots, made their way to the river, Haseya stopped and looked at the old woman.

After a few seconds of eye contact, Ch'agii transformed into a coyote. Haseya felt a thunk at her feet as her brother dropped his water pot. As the Ch'agii-coyote slowly moved toward them, he grabbed and her arm. 'Come on! Come on! We must go back to the village!'

But Haseya shook her loose from his grip. 'I will say the name,' she said. 'I am unafraid. I will rise.'

The coyote lumbered forward, closer and closer. Haseya's brother, with a final whimper of panic, ran away. But Haseya held her ground.

Closer and closer came the Ch'agii-coyote. So close, that its snout was only inches from Haseya's nose. Haseya could smell rotted flesh – she noticed bits of skin and dried blood around the coyote's muzzle. Staring deep into its eyes, she proclaimed, 'I name you, creature; I name you Ch'agii!'

The Ch'agii-coyote whipped her head up to the sky and howled. 'Ch'agii!' Haseya called out again, in triumph.

The Ch'agii-coyote leapt upon Haseya, ripping flesh from bone. Ch'agii-coyote sunk her head into the girl's stomach, and began shredding the delicate organs within. By the time the men from the village arrived, the Ch'agii-coyote had disappeared, leaving only a pile of blood and viscera by the riverbank.

The men gathered the remains for the ceremonial burning, as the women and children wept. Haseya's mother held tight to her remaining child.

'You must always cast down your eyes!'

BEAUTY, LIES, SLEEPING

BILL HUGHES

'The same pressures that bind with briars a woman's joys and desires are the pressures that will destroy the world' (Germaine Greer)

Starved stringy dogs yelled at us, snapping at the heels of my horse, then cringed back as I cursed them. Otherwise, the town was stagnant in the noon heat. No curious faces peered out from the dark doorways, or slyly opened shutters to gawp at my arrival. Dust lay over the low stone huts and the forest shadowed the hills to the back of the town with an uneasy greenness.

I dismounted in the centre of the town where a water-trough stood. I led the weary animal there, and he gratefully bent his head and drank the dark dubious water. I also bent to try and wash off the hot dust and the sweat of the past nights. Lately I had slept little for fear of being drenched again with the mounting nightmares that had ridden me out to these desolate lands.

The horse moved with a sharp pointing of his ears. Sleep-thirsty nerves, tautened by the strangeness of this place, jerked me around, bright sword in hand. A child of about eight, dressed in a shabby grey frock, stared at me with large terrified eyes. She was thin as the dogs, and seemed as dried-up and dust-ridden as everything in this petrified town. I tried to calm her from my parched throat—her dark fear-filled eyes accused me in some way—but the resultant croak sent her scurrying away.

*

Sleep, to extinguish the roar of words, dissolve through the façade and gestate in a deep pool of formless potential. The hard constructs of necessity are walled away by soft eyelids, trembling as the black sleeping eyes wander rapidly to and fro. Down here, the swimming instincts alone are at play, crazed and unhindered.

She, I, is a little girl, running wild through room after room in this infinite house, opening doors. Rich brown hair and dark excited eyes, dreaming. Then, astonished, these eyes wonder at the marvellous tapestry hung in this last room I have discovered. Golden thread is spun through it, and velvety purples; azure and brilliant greens and crimsons. A world wheels there, spinning visions of immensity and liberty. She is running through the luxurious meadows pictured there; both a part of the legend and the author of it. My body is burning with pleasure. I swim in cool lakes. I plunge into the tangle of an exciting forest. Suddenly the frame confines me: it is pressing the breath out of me. A sharp pricking in my thumbs. A cry; the clatter of arms; there is blood on that drab domesticated piece of needlework.

*

The horse stood patiently as I tethered him to a tree. I had ridden up the stony track to the forest, which seemed to menace me more and more as I approached. Its gnarled intricacies held the secret of my nightmares. My sleep had been choked with images of snakish woods, with boughs that bled as I forced my way through them to kill the witch that lurked at their centre.

Wise men had shown me histories which placed my dreams in this reality where I now stood; hesitant.

I began to penetrate the forest, hacking angrily away at the branches with my sword. The joy of the fight entered me; I shouted my ancestral name, hurling it as a battle-cry to assert my self over this silent obscure darkness which lay passive but threatening before me. The wood fell easily to my glimmering blade.

Hours passed; the darkness deepened as night began to fall and I grew weary. The dank heat of the air, filled with bark dust, unmanned me. Black gritty flecks stuck to my sweating flesh and my limbs weakened. Fear descended suddenly upon me; the air chilled. A bird shrieked; a strange call, like that of a girl. Then a hint of grey through the gloomy trees and I stumbled forth into a marble courtyard, aged by neglect.

*

There are cooks, lovers, shepherds, musicians, cattle, mid-wives, jewellers, hounds, poets, astronomers, two cats, a weaver, dress-makers, watch-makers, athletes, clowns and madmen here, all sleeping.

She is coming, commingling, in this bed where silks caress the skin, where liquid velvet thoughts breed in the depths of my body. Strands of chestnut hair criss-cross my eager breasts, weave a pattern on this body which is travelling through strangely wooded landscapes, stroked by satin foliages. What has lain dormant is gathering momentum, moving towards arousal. Secretions, dreams, manifest themselves to coerce the world into their shape. A brutal loudness splinters this fragility.

*

A man, stale with sweat and black grime, is standing in the doorway to my chamber. His face is weary, fearful, vicious—perhaps courageous. I am afraid, too; my skin flinches from imagined blows, ruptures. But I face him defiantly, my nakedness against his leather jerkin, his stupid sword, the cruel constricting boots. He laughs.

When I first saw that naked beauty my blood thickened—I wanted to rape her, to make her bleed under my will. Then I felt a sudden revulsion at myself, at my laughter. It seemed crude, too loud, in this scented alcove with its silken weavings. I had laughed out of triumph, relief, disdain at the frailness of this evil, caught lying vulnerable to my sword. But I laughed also from unease at the disparity between this sensuous form and the cold murderousness of my dreams. I remembered again the wise men, the old books, the ritual violations that my ancestors had performed against her. I saw her eyes were open and upon me.

He knelt before me. And I laughed back at him then, of course! That dolt wallowing in humility and guilt. And seeing the coarse rage in him wilt to self-degradation stirred harshness in me. Spittle and venom formed under my tongue.

Sadism, that desperate clutching at identity, security, surrenders as I fall into an abyss of namelessness. Words fall away from the world. The structures I had so carefully wrought around and within me crumble dizzily before the onslaught of her dark candid gaze.

It could not have reasonably been otherwise. The desire was not strong and, despite the tenderness I felt at the tears that wetted his cheeks, distaste still lingered. But that long sleep of dreams had to end. He, this lumbering clod with his sword and savage ways, was needed to awaken me, as I had awoken the living gentleness in him. Freedom lay naked upon his face; cruelty and his sword abandoned. I invited him over to my bed. Uneasy embraces; then we merge; not invasion, nor engulfment; we sweat and cry out, one body stiffens as one grows fierce and then we lie in a passionate stillness; recreated.

*

A clear wakefulness has composed everything. Madrigals are being sung and steaming pastries of all sorts perfume the fired ovens. Animals and children shout through the palace as the clowns tumble and the lunatics perform their masques. Armed, I dance down through the flowering forest to where the thirsty world waits.

The Natural Order of Things

Barry Hall

The forest is old and purple-green. There is a smell of candy. Thin mist like a gauzy nightgown; dew on the leaves, and moonlight in shafts mark the way.

'Don't run far!' they call. And she doesn't. Nor would I expect her to. Not yet. In another season or two.

I have turned from that path though. Deep in the woods. There is laughter in the village, and the warm soft light of candles, the smell of baking bread, and once upon a time.

*

Snow covers the forest. Pale blue winter. I am lean as the willow and as cold. The butcher's corpse will steam in the chill night; eviscerated and rose red on the snow. His taste will be rich and iron as claret. And when the men come, wild-eyed and shitting with terror, they will be far from the path and I will be gone.

*

Damp gnaws at my bones. I am failing.

*

Dark moss underfoot. The drizzle chills the silent forest, trapped in the lace of web in the willow. I remember a half-glimpsed blue faerie girl in diaphanous silk; her hair was black as the witching hour. But ivy has grown wild over the cottage. And there is a low-walled garden. Even the garden has a path. There's sadness here. And solitude. Ghosts in the moonlight.

I can see her through the window inside. Bent and scowling. Thin lips drawn back over ruined teeth, and she strains as she pulls the skin from a rabbit. There's a pot of carrots and barley on the range. A bloody knife.

'Oh my...' the old woman's whisper twisted as the roots of the old willow at the crossroads.

'What big eyes you have.'   Indeed!

Figure 25 Carnivorous Porkers

FEAR LITTLE PIGGY

LAURA KREMMEL

Jerry was my patient and friend, and he came to see me several times before his unfortunate demise. The story is wrong. Pigs do eat bones and they did eat his, but they weren't his pigs.

They told him not to buy a book from the turret in the tower in woods. All the people at Forest Lodge, that is, where he had been staying for the weekend. Jerry never ventured far from home for long; he had too many animals to take care of. Everyone knew about the tower in the woods where old man Rusket lived selling furniture in his shop. Going there meant crossing a little bridge like in a fairy tale. The ground around the tower always saturated to a dense and sticky mud, a mixture of slippery leaves grown wet and decaying; something about a natural spring that ran right under the building's foundation.

The old man kept four or five piglets, kept them all on one leash like dogs and paraded them around the woods every morning before the sun came up. They were his children—so Jerry told me—and so he called them his own pigs. Everyone knew about the even older man, who lived in the tower above Rusket, with all his old, old books. Books that could be yours— for the right price. The bookshop was in the turret in the tower.

'Don't go to it', they warned him.

Jerry went to it.

Jerry had never been a reader. I can't explain what he was doing there. Hoping to see the man walking his pigs, maybe? All I know is he showed up in my office the next day, a bandage slouching off his temples, held in place by a brown blood stain. He was carrying a book-shaped plastic-bag-covered bundle, away from his body like it was a sack of garbage.

'I need you to look at something,' he said. 'It's an injury.' I nodded and started to remove his bandage. 'But it's not my injury'

And then he told me about the tower.

'I found the staircase by accident,' he said. 'My feet climbed the first few steps just to get a look at it but then they kept moving, pulled trippingly up and up and into darkness until CRACK, my head hit on a low ceiling. I fell headlong through a door and into a room, even darker than the stairwell. Opening my eyes wide, I felt blind from the blow, until someone standing right in front of me struck a match. A dancing flame painted a face at the level of my chest. The face smiled and looked down at a few glistening spots on the floor. I opened my mouth to speak, but it came out as a SLAM. The face had thrown a bible-sized tome over the spots on the floor. 'Much better,' it said. 'Would you care for a book?'

'I was feeling faint from inhaling smoke and fire and darkness; drunk on invisibility and the throbbing in my head. 'Any books about animals? Do you know of any?'

"'I should', he said. 'I wrote them all.' His face appeared and disappeared; disembodied as a balloon. 'Place your hand just… here,' he said, taking my arm away from my broken head and guiding it by the elbow.

'I felt a row of spines like a catacomb, curving my fingers up and over and clawing one down into my arms. 'How much do I owe you?' My speech was starting to slur.

"'Oh. I think you've already paid,' said the face from somewhere and then the room blacked out.

'So, Doc, I got this book here. A gift, I guess, but… I think there's something wrong with it. It's sick or it's hurt itself or something.'

He started to unwrap it, layer after layer and then the paint appeared, a little at first so I thought that it was just the effect of the plastic, but then clearly the layers came off damp, then dripping with thick red. Had he gotten it wet? Had the dyes from the cover and the glues from the pages sopped into a goo? It was so very red.

'Can you help it, Doc? Do you think it hurts?'

The bloody thing was bleeding.

'I took it home with me the next morning to have a good look at it,' he said. 'I was about to flip through it, see if there were in fact any stories about animals in it, when I heard my little ones calling to me from the yard, the little oink oinks. They're so hungry in the morning. How could I forget them? I fear I was too tired and too clumsy that night to handle the book. The first time I turned the page, a thin rip screeched right down the middle.' He gently pried the covers open against their sticky suction and unglued the first page, barely still solid, the pulp visible through the two-inch tear. 'And that's when it started bleeding,' Jerry said. 'There used to be words. I was just wondering if, maybe if you cured it, the words might come back.'

Hesitant to touch the mushy mass myself, I stretched on a pair of gloves, and cracked the spine halfway through. I couldn't help but wonder at how warm it was. Curiously, as soggy as the book was, the last page was dry as a bone, but it was blank.

I wanted the disgusting thing out of my office. I wanted it as far away as possible. I threw some gauze at Jerry and pushed him and his book out the door. 'Wrap this around it,' I said. 'Try to stop the bleeding.'

Two weeks later he was back, red-faced and blubbering. This time with a new book clutched to his chest but he was still dripping, a bulge of bandage wrapped around his right index finger. 'I killed them, Doc. I can't believe I killed them! My babies!'

It was half an hour and a shot of whisky before I could get more words out of him than that. 'I was wrapping the book, like you said. I was trying to keep the one healthy page clean and dry when my hand slipped and the edge of the page sliced down my finger. I've had paper cuts before and worse, but nothing that's bled like that and it hasn't stopped. At least the book is cured though.'

He placed it on the table, a medium-sized hardback, completely dry; clean pages, not even water-damaged. I picked it up and flipped through. Blank. A journal.

'This can't be the same book,' I said.

'The last time I wrapped it, I must have done it really well, but I don't want it! I want my babies!'

'Calm down, Jerry. What happened to your pigs?'

'I didn't mean to do it! But I couldn't stand it! After I cut my finger I wrapped it up, but it wouldn't stop bleeding. I had to do the chores. I couldn't not feed my babies. While I was pouring the slop in their pen, some of the blood got mixed in. I told them not to eat it, but the little oink oinks slurped it up. I didn't think it would actually hurt them. When I was making my dinner, I heard them squealing under the window, oinking at me louder than I've ever heard. They had slipped out of the pen and followed me to the house. I put them back and explained to them how nice their little pen home was. But that night they got into the house, oinking at the top of their little voices. It wouldn't stop. They followed me everywhere for days and days. All I could hear was the oinking, oinking, louder and louder. It seemed like there were hundreds of them all around me; in my head. I couldn't take it, Doc! Couldn't take it! I didn't want to do it!'

'There, there, Jerry. You have plenty of other animals to look after. You can get some new pigs.'

'It hasn't stopped.'

'What?'

'The oinking hasn't stopped. It followed me down the hallway to your office. It's waiting for me out there. I don't know what to do about that…' He held up his finger. '… Or about this.'

'Jerry,' I said. 'I think you need to return that book.'

And that was the last time I saw or heard from Jerry. It wasn't until I heard some of his animals had gotten loose that I started looking. I called all his relatives, his friends, checked with all the farmers markets and state fairs. Nothing. It was days later that I thought to call the Forest Lodge. He had checked in soon after he had left my office and had gone out that evening. He had not returned his key to the hotel. They had a strict policy.

I don't know why I didn't wait until morning to go out there. It wasn't until nearly sunrise that I found myself standing on the little bridge. I stood, twisting backwards, trying to see any windows that might give me a clue. I had been concentrating so hard that it was a minute or so before I heard the snorting. The old man was taking his piglets out for their nightly walk, letting them wade way out into the sludge around the tower. I stood and watched them, unseen above in the dim light. Cute. Jerry would have loved them.

That's when I heard the 'slop slop slop' turn into a 'CRUNCH crunch crunch' and I stared into the darkness, trying to see what they had gotten their snouts into. When the old man and his pets left, I crept off the bridge, stepping gingerly into the leaves and mud, poking my foot around for the source of the crunch. Just as the sun came up, I found it.

Bones.

The ground was littered with bones, half sticking up, half buried, all shapes and sizes, some alarmingly large. I did not want to know what animal had died there. Or, how many.

I walked quickly back to the Lodge, trying along the way to shuffle off the muck and leaves sticking to my shoes. By the time I arrived, the sun was fully up and shining brightly. I sat down and took off one of my shoes. The mud was redder than I had ever seen, and I stopped scraping when I noticed they were not leaves sticking to my heel. They were pages, sodden and stained. I had seen something like them before.

When the police called, I told them to check out the farm. When the reporters called, I told them the same. Turns out the reason Jerry's finger wouldn't stop bleeding was because one of the pigs had actually bitten off part of it with the bone. They found fragments... somehow. However, they find anything. So they think his pigs killed him... never mind that the pigs themselves are dead. That's wilful blindness. I'm certainly not going to correct them.

Figure 26 Extreme Piggy Close-up

EVIL-ALICE

JENAH COLLEDGE

There was never 'Once Upon a Time',
It's only horror within this rhyme.
Dining at the table, kicking her feet,
White fur shawl and pie to eat.
Golden hair and mad-hatter mind,
This girl was twisted and far from kind.
She carved with care and gutted with style,
Wiped the blood from her mouth, once in a while.
The pile of insides, a centre piece,
Honouring those who were deceased.
Smiling wide from ear to ear, triumphant with her work,
Razor teeth and feline claws, in her land where evil lurks.
Admiring her view over delicious gore tart,
She really was the queen of hearts.

If only it was a child in dream,
not a repetitive terror for those who'd seen.
Whilst in her trance, her prison, her hell,
They were actually pushed
those that fell.
All it took was a gentle touch,
To enter her hellish rabbit hutch.
Knives and blood, a tea party of flesh,
Trapped within Gothic wilderness.
When removed from tight grasp on the hospital ward,
Her visitors in deadlights, admitted with cause.
The story runs on with no end, and centuries pass amongst silent cries,
And for every time the tale is told...
Another white rabbit dies.

Figure 27 Evil Alice

RUINS

ANDREA BOWD

Stoic gaze from cracked, veined eyes
in a stately home with crumbling walls,
wrapped in ivy, no-one calls.
Rooks glide past as pale wind sighs.

Oak and ash meet crumbling stone.
Yew trees frame at time's bequest,
entomb brick in wreathed caress.
Emerald moss adds her soft tone.

Where the living no more dwell
a footstep treads as light as breath.
A soul which fails to bow to death,
sees splendour in the ruined shell.

A lonely realm of sad decay
remains in wraiths of twisted time.
Where nature claims freedom divine,
and grace suspended greets the day

FINIS

Figure 28 Memento Mori

… and they all lived happily ever after!

NOTES ON CONTRIBUTORS

Figure 29 Madness

Editor
Colin Younger ('Once upon a Tyne') is Programme Leader for English Literature and Creative Writing at the University of Sunderland. A published poet, song-writer and scholar of Borders Theory, his works include *Border Crossings: Narration, Nation and Imagination in Scots and Irish Literature and Culture* (2013), *Spectral Visions: The Collection* (2014) and *Borders Gothic and the Folkloric Vampire* (2016).

Foreword
Iain Rowan is Assistant Director of Academic Services at the University of Sunderland and a published author. His publications include *One of Us* (2006), which was shortlisted for the Crime Writers' Association Debut Dagger award, *Nowhere to Go* (2011) and *Ice Age* (2013), and he has sold over thirty short stories to various publications. Iain is the founder of Sunderland's Holmeside Writers Group.

Cover
David Newton provides graphic design for Spectral Visions Press. He studied Clinical Biochemistry and Computing at Northumbria University and has worked in the NHS and IT Management. He founded Road Ahead Music and Media in 2009; it may be visited at www.roadaheadmedia.com

Illustrator
Katie Lloyd has a degree in Graphics Communication from South Tyneside College. She now works in the University of Sunderland libraries. Her portfolio page may be viewed at facebook.com/misskittykegs

Mike Adamson ('The Tale of the Black Knight and the White Princess') holds a PhD in archaeology from Flinders University of South Australia, where he teaches. Mike is a passionate photographer and a master-level hobbyist who writes for international magazines, and his academic work has appeared through Cambridge University Press and the University of Sunderland Press.

Emily Bird ('An Overturned Tale') is a third-year English & Creative Writing student at the University of Sunderland. She has previously been published in *Once Upon a Rhyme: Northern England Volume 2*. Her writing may be viewed at abookwormandbooklover.blogspot.co.uk

Andrea Bowd ('Ruins') holds a BA (Hons) in Creative Writing from the University of Nottingham, and is soon to start her MA in English Literature, also at Nottingham.

Joseph Brash ('Reverie') is a second-year English & Creative Writing student at the University of Sunderland.

Jenah Colledge ('Evil-Alice') is a third-year BA (Hons) student at the University of Sunderland. She has had two articles published on the Spectral Visions blog: *Twisty the Clown* and *To Whom Does Control Belong?*

Emma Collingwood ('Love and Death') is a graduate of Northumbria University, where she studied French and Business. Her creative writing specialities are fairy tales and historical fiction.

Janet Cooper ('A Family Dinner') holds a BA (Hons) in English & Creative Writing from the University of Sunderland, where she is currently an MA student. She has been published in *Spectral Visions: The Collection* (2014). Her work may be viewed at janetcooper.webs.com

Jade Diamond ('The Witch of Hardknot Pass') is a third-year English & Creative Writing student at the University of Sunderland.

Daniel Farrell ('The Glass Coffin') is a third year English student at the University of Sunderland. He is working on his second novel.

Stephanie Gallon ('Wolfbann') holds a BA (Hons) in English & Creative Writing from the University of Sunderland, where she is currently an MA student. She has been published in *North East Writers Sampler Volume 2* and *Material* magazine. Her work may be viewed at stephanieanngallon.wix.com/writing

Charlotte Haley ('The Princess and the Pea') is a student at Grindon Hall Christian School. She has been published in her school magazine, *Probo 2013*.

Barry Hall ('The Natural Order of Things') is an English lecturer at the University of Sunderland and a member of the North East Forum in Eighteenth-Century and Romantic Studies. His publications include: *Conflict, Closure, Dilemma: Bunyan's Grace Abounding* (2013).

Ashleigh Hallimond ('Midnight') holds a BA in English & Creative Writing and an MA in English Literature from the University of Sunderland. She is working on her as-yet-untitled Young Adult novel.

Bill Hughes ('beauty, lies, sleeping') holds a PhD in English Literature from the University of Sheffield. His research and publications explore the interrelation of the dialogue genre and English novels of the long eighteenth century. Bill has also published on Richard Hoggart, intertextuality, and the Semantic Web, and contemporary paranormal romance. He is co-organiser, with Dr Sam George, of the Open Graves, Open Minds: Vampires and the Undead in Modern Culture Project at the University of Hertfordshire and co-editor (with Dr George) of *'Open Graves, Open Minds': Vampires and the Undead from the Enlightenment to the Present* (2013). He is on the editorial board of the journal *Monstrum*.

Laura Kremmel ('Fear Little Piggy') is a PhD candidate at Lehigh University in Pennsylvania; her dissertation examines Romantic-Era Gothic Literature, Gothic Bodies, and History of Medicine. She blogs for several Gothic and Romanticism blogs, runs a Gothic reading group, and has a publication on *The Walking Dead*.

Erica Little-Gainford ('The Baroness and the Servant Girl') holds a BA (Hons) in Ancient History and Archaeology from the University of Reading. Her final year dissertation was on the origins and evolution of vampire superstition, and burial evidence of these myths.

Michelle McCabe ('Dragon') is a third-year English and Creative Writing student at the University of Sunderland. Her short story 'Laura' was published in *Spectral Visions: The Collection* (2014).

Gary McKay ('Jack the Giant Butcher') holds a BA (Hons) and an MRes in English from the University of Ulster.

Alex Milne ('The Ghost Who Died') is an investment banker in New York, originally from Edinburgh. His novels and stories are inspired by fairy tales and the supernatural. He has had short fiction published online at dooreditch.co.uk and txtlit.co.uk, where he is a former winner of the monthly competition.

Sophie Raine ('Choke') holds a BA in English & Creative Writing and an MA in English Literature from the University of Sunderland. Her main area of interest within English studies is Gothic Literature, specifically looking at the Gothic in relation to feminism and consumerism. She has written for the Spectral Visions blog.

Jamie Spears ('Cast Down Your Eyes') is an English Literature PhD student at the University of Sunderland. Her research interests include the Gothic, Spiritualism and Theosophy, the New Woman and the Long Nineteenth Century. Recent publications have appeared in *The Criterion, Evil, Woman and the Feminine*, and *Spectral Visions: The Collection* (2014). She writes at worldofthegothic.blogspot.co.uk

James Strachan ('The Tree') is a Bohemian Polyglot and a student of English at Royal Holloway, University of London. He enjoys reading De Sade and composing short stories, poems and operas.

John Strachan ('The Story of Iron Henry') is Professor of English at Bath Spa University. He has previously taught at the universities of Northumbria, Oxford and Sunderland. His poetry has appeared in several magazines and collections, including *Spectral Visions: The Collection* (2014). He is also widely published in academic and scholarly fields.

Glen Supple ('From the Sky') has worked as an actor and theatre director, and is the author of several short plays, some of which have been produced on London's Fringe. His fiction focuses on the supernatural.

Jennie Watson ('Sweet Red') is a third-year BA English & Drama student at the University of Sunderland. She writes poetry at jennkapow.wordpress.com

Joshua Wray ('The Elfin-song') holds a BA in Philosophy, and is soon to start his MA in Gothic Literature at Manchester Metropolitan University. He is working on his second Gothic Romance novel, a sequel, *Fletcher: Volume II*.

Alison Younger ('The Huldrefolk' and 'Little Red Riding Blood') is Programme Leader for MA English Studies at the University of Sunderland. An extremely talented critical and creative writer, her publications include: *Representing Ireland: Past, Present and Future*, (2005), *Essays on Modern Irish Literature*, (2007), *Ireland at War and Peace* (2011), *No Country for Old Men: Fresh Perspectives on Irish Literature* (2008), *Celtic Connections: Irish-Scottish Relations and the Politics of Culture* (2012) and *Spectral Visions: The Collection* (2014).

Printed in Great Britain
by Amazon.co.uk, Ltd.,
Marston Gate.